FINAL DESCENT

Frank banked the ultralight airplane, preparing to circle back to the homestead. Suddenly he felt a jerk on his right foot pedal, and the ultralight whipped into a spin.

Frank frantically worked the rudder pedals. The right one was stuck in the stop position. Trying the left pedal, he managed to move it slightly—but then it stuck, too.

Fighting panic, Frank glanced behind him at the tail. The rudder was definitely jammed, which meant that a cable must have broken and the control line had fouled.

The ultralight kept whirling in a tight circle—and the ground was moving up closer and closer.

If Frank didn't get control back, the ultralight would crash!

Books in THE HARDY BOYS CASEFILES® Series

#1 DEAD ON TARGET
#2 EVIL, INC.
#3 CULT OF CRIME
#4 THE LAZARUS PLOT
#5 EDGE OF DESTRUCTION
#6 THE CROWNING TERROR
#7 DEATHGAME
#8 SEE NO EVIL
#9 THE GENIUS THIEVES
#10 HOSTAGES OF HATE
#11 BROTHER AGAINST BROTHER
#12 PERFECT GETAWAY
#13 THE BORGIA DAGGER
#14 TOO MANY TRAITORS
#15 BLOOD RELATIONS
#16 LINE OF FIRE
#17 THE NUMBER FILE
#18 A KILLING IN THE MARKET
#19 NIGHTMARE IN ANGEL CITY
#20 WITNESS TO MURDER
#21 STREET SPIES
#22 DOUBLE EXPOSURE
#23 DISASTER FOR HIRE
#24 SCENE OF THE CRIME
#25 THE BORDERLINE CASE
#26 TROUBLE IN THE PIPELINE
#27 NOWHERE TO RUN
#28 COUNTDOWN TO TERROR
#29 THICK AS THIEVES
#30 THE DEADLIEST DARE
#31 WITHOUT A TRACE
#32 BLOOD MONEY
#33 COLLISION COURSE
#34 FINAL CUT
#35 THE DEAD SEASON
#36 RUNNING ON EMPTY
#37 DANGER ZONE
#38 DIPLOMATIC DECEIT
#39 FLESH AND BLOOD
#40 FRIGHT WAVE
#41 HIGHWAY ROBBERY

Available from ARCHWAY Paperbacks

Most Archway Paperbacks are available at special quantity discounts for bulk purchases for sales promotions, premiums or fund raising. Special books or book excerpts can also be created to fit specific needs.

For details write the office of the Vice President of Special Markets, Pocket Books, 1230 Avenue of the Americas, New York, New York 10020.

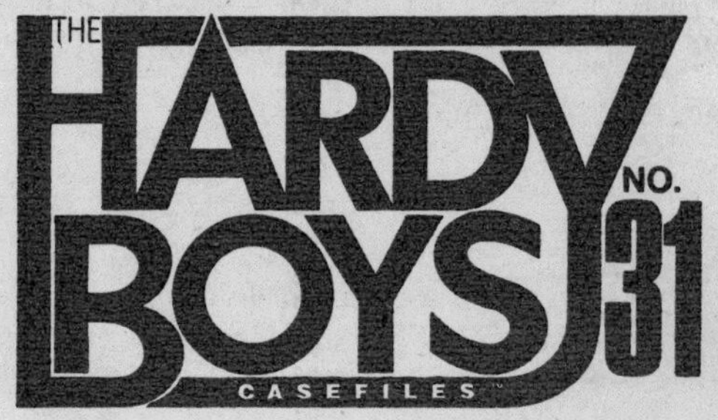

WITHOUT A TRACE

FRANKLIN W. DIXON

AN ARCHWAY PAPERBACK
Published by POCKET BOOKS
New York London Toronto Sydney Tokyo Singapore

This book is a work of fiction. Names, characters, places and incidents are either the product of the author's imagination or are used fictitiously. Any resemblance to actual events or locales or persons, living or dead, is entirely coincidental.

AN ARCHWAY PAPERBACK *Original*

An Archway Paperback published by
POCKET BOOKS, a division of Simon & Schuster Inc.
1230 Avenue of the Americas, New York, NY 10020

Copyright © 1989 by Simon & Schuster Inc.
Cover art copyright © 1989 Brian Kotzky
Produced by Mega-Books of New York, Inc.

All rights reserved, including the right to reproduce this book or portions thereof in any form whatsoever. For information address Pocket Books, 1230 Avenue of the Americas, New York, NY 10020

ISBN: 0-671-67479-X

First Archway Paperback printing September 1989

10 9 8 7 6 5 4 3 2

THE HARDY BOYS, AN ARCHWAY PAPERBACK and colophon are registered trademarks of Simon & Schuster Inc.

THE HARDY BOYS CASEFILES is a trademark of Simon & Schuster Inc.

Printed in the U.S.A.

IL 7+

WITHOUT A TRACE

Chapter 1

"I *HATE* TINY PLANES!" Joe Hardy's face was pale under his blond hair as the small commuter plane dipped in midair. Joe looked as if his stomach had been left on the ceiling.

Across the aisle, lean, brown-haired Frank Hardy grinned. "Cool it, Joe. If you settle down and look out the window, I bet you'll see Lubbock. We'll be on the ground in minutes, and then at the ranch in a couple of hours—if our ride's waiting for us."

"Great," Joe growled. "We limp over half of Texas in this oversize eggbeater and then have to drive the rest of the way to New Mexico. A nice, big jet would have gotten us there much faster."

Frank shrugged. "Not the way the schedules run. And look how much more you're seeing than you did on the jet from Bayport to Dallas." He grinned. "And you don't get the *feel* of flying in a jet. You might as well be riding an elevator."

Just then the small craft lurched, buffeted by rising warm air.

Joe's knuckles were white as he gripped the arms of his seat. "Right—this really beats flying in a nice, comfortable jet with cushy seats." He glanced out the window. "Ever since you got your student pilot's license and started to solo, all I hear from you is flying." He turned back from the window. "At least we don't have to worry about plowing into a mountain. It's flat as a tabletop."

Frank glanced briefly out the window. "Yeah, I bet even I could make an emergency landing down there if I had to."

Joe shook his head. "I hope the scenery improves in New Mexico. Doesn't sound like it, though, does it? I'm not excited to be looking at a few dead cows. I must have missed something—why isn't the local sheriff handling this, or the vet?"

"The cows belong to Roy Carlson, and Dad owes him a favor," Frank said as if he'd told him before. "And it's more than a few dead cattle. Roy isn't a guy to lose his cool easily. Anybody who runs a ranch the size of his—fifty thousand acres—" He stopped. "They're reducing power. We're on the final approach to Lubbock."

The plane banked steeply. Joe saw the runway pavement crisscrossing a field ahead. To the west, the sky was turning a dirty brown.

"Looks like we're coming into a dust storm," Frank said. The twin-engine plane bounced lightly on the cement as it touched down, taxied down the runway, and stopped. The Hardys waited while the copilot got their bags. Then they crossed the pavement and entered Lubbock Terminal.

"Frank? Joe?" A woman's voice called out.

They turned to see a tiny, older woman, wearing jeans and an embroidered western shirt, with snow white hair piled high on her head.

Frank smiled. "We're the Hardys."

"I'm Dot Carlson, Roy's wife." She extended her small hand to grip Frank's, which to Frank's surprise was firm and strong. "Roy's sorry that he couldn't pick you up." She lowered her voice. "We've got another problem at the ranch."

"What kind of problem?" Joe asked.

"I'll tell you in the car," Dot said. Minutes later the boys' bags were in the trunk of a large white luxury car. Frank sat in the front seat beside Dot, and Joe in the rear. Almost as soon as they left the parking lot, they were in open country. Ahead of them, the storm spread across the western sky like a huge brown stain.

"I don't like the looks of that dust storm." Dot frowned. "It'll hamper the search."

Frank raised his eyebrows. "Search?"

"Roy and Rudy are out looking for Jerry Greene. He didn't show up for work this morning." Dot sounded worried.

"Maybe he's just taking a long weekend," Joe suggested.

"Jerry's not like that," Dot said. "His father worked for Roy for thirty years, and Jerry's always treated the ranch as if it were his own. He's been coming up with all sorts of new ideas to run the ranch better." She smiled. "He's just a little older than you boys. In fact, he's more like a grandson than an employee. No, I'm afraid it's more trouble."

"Who's Rudy?" Frank asked.

"Rudy Castillo is our other hand," Dot replied.

"You mean, Roy ranches fifty thousand acres with only two hands?" Joe blurted out in disbelief.

Dot nodded, amused. "*You* may think the Circle C is big, but it takes hundreds of acres of this rough country to feed one steer. If we need more hands, we borrow them from other ranchers." Her smile faded. "Ranching isn't going through boom times right now. Even some really big spreads went under when the price of beef dropped."

"This is where the dead cattle come in?" Joe asked.

Dot sighed. "Roy will give you the details. But it looks like somebody's trying to drive us out of business. Roy's been trying to get to the bottom of it, but so far, no luck. We hope you can help."

The dust storm was sweeping over them now, cutting the visibility to a few hundred feet. Swirls of fine soil rippled across the road. After a while they passed a sign that read, Welcome to New Mexico, Land of Enchantment, but it was almost obscured by blowing dust.

Frank grinned. "Do these storms happen often?" he asked.

"Too often," Dot said, concentrating on the road as they continued to drive west. "This is a hard land—no trees to break the wind, no surface water. The Spanish who settled Santa Fe over three hundred years ago called the area *La Tierra Encantada*. State boosters translate it to mean 'enchanted,' but the words also mean 'the bewitched land.' All this open territory pretty much belonged to the Indians and the comancheros—renegade whites—until after the Civil War."

More miles passed. Finally they pulled up to a run-down gas station and parked beside a dirty, once-red pickup truck. "Where are we?" Joe asked, peering through the fine haze of dust that whirled and covered everything.

Dot laughed. "This is the 'town' of Caprock—gas station, post office, and general store. I'm going to pick up the mail. We still have some distance to go." She stepped from the car and with her head down bolted for the door.

The boys watched her disappear inside. When she started to come out, her hands full of mail, a giant of a man walked up and blocked her exit. With his broken nose and big hands, he towered threateningly over her. But all he did was give her a surprisingly sweet smile and hold the door for her.

They talked for a moment, then Dot darted back to the car. The giant headed for the pickup with a fancy gun rack in its cab.

"Who *was* that guy?" Joe asked curiously when Dot got back into the car.

Dot was smiling. "He's the new foreman at the Triple O—Nat Wilkin. I hope his boss doesn't hear about him being polite to me. We've had trouble with Oscar Owens, the owner, off and on for years—and we'll have more. Nat just warned me that Oscar's upset about a fence being down." She started the car and backed onto the road.

"Do most people carry guns around here?" Frank asked.

Dot shrugged. "There's a bounty on coyotes. You can't tell when you'll meet one."

"Why is the town called Caprock?" Joe asked as they continued their westbound drive.

"You'd see the caprock shortly," Dot answered, "if it weren't for this storm. It's a long cliff that runs for miles, north to south. On the east side of it, where we are now, is the *Llano Estacado*—the 'Staked Plains.' It's almost perfectly flat, and the story is that the Indians marked their trails with stakes because there weren't any other landmarks. To the west are the sand hills—" Suddenly a gust of wind rocked the car, and she struggled for control.

"Hey!" Joe exclaimed, staring out the window. "Did you see that guy?"

"What guy?" Frank asked. "Anybody'd have to be crazy to be out in *this*." He peered out the window. "I can't see anything."

"But *I* saw him," Joe insisted. "An old geezer with a Mexican hat and some sort of straw bag. One minute he was standing there, and the next minute he just seemed to vanish."

"Must have been Caprock Charlie," Dot suggested, the car under control again. "Some folks think he's Native American, some Mexican, but most say he's loco. You know," she said, tapping the side of her head, "touched. He appears out of nowhere at the oddest times."

Dot turned off the highway and onto a dirt

road. "Almost there," she said. Through the swirling dust they could just make out a low, white-painted stucco ranch house with a cedar-shingle roof. They pulled up beside several pickups parked in front.

A tall man with a weathered face, around sixty, opened the front door and stepped out. He wore a jacket and a light gray Stetson. "So these are Fenton's boys, eh?" he said. "Welcome to the Circle C. I'm Roy Carlson."

"I'm Frank. This is Joe," Frank told him, shaking hands.

"Any sign of Jerry?" Dot asked worriedly.

"Nope," Roy replied. "We just got back from his bunkhouse. Looks like he left in a big hurry—food on the table, TV still on, the truck out front. But his horse is gone, so he must've ridden out. I figured we wouldn't have much luck tracking him in this storm. I did call the sheriff, and he'll be out soon." He looked at Frank. "You know anything about telephone answering machines?"

Frank grinned. "A little. What do you want to know?"

"Will you excuse us?" Ray asked Dot. He led the way into a small office. An answering machine sat on the desk, its red light blinking. "Jerry set this up yesterday, but I wasn't here before he had to leave, so he didn't explain how it works. Now I'm afraid I'll make the stupid thing erase itself." Outside, a horn sounded, and Roy turned. "Maybe that's the sheriff." He hurried out the door.

Frank looked the machine over, then pressed a button. The tape whirred. "Hi, Roy," a cheerful voice said. "This is Jerry. I'm back at the bunkhouse and I thought I'd give the machine a try. See you in the morning." The message ended with a loud beep.

Then a second message came on. "Roy! This is Jerry." The ranch hand sounded worried. "It's ten o'clock, and there's something weird going on near the old homestead. I can see lights. I'm going down to have a look."

Frank and Joe stared at each other. Was this a lead to Jerry's whereabouts? Suddenly they were aware of angry voices out front, loud and getting louder.

A threatening voice cut above Roy's, shouting, "I want that fence fixed and I want it fixed pronto. I'm warning you, Carlson. The next critter—four- or *two*-legged—that wanders onto my place is going to be buzzard bait!"

Chapter 2

As Frank and Joe dashed to the front of the ranch house, they heard the slam of a door, the roar of a powerful engine, and the sound of tires sliding on gravel. They reached the porch just in time to see a shiny pickup speed off.

"Who was that?" Frank asked Roy, who was calmly watching the pickup disappear into the dust storm.

"Oscar Owens," Roy said. "He owns the Triple O, just south of us." He shook his head. "That old boy's got a short fuse, but he'll get over it. Always does."

"What was he mad about?" Joe asked, trailing the others back into the house.

"His foreman spotted some of my cattle on his land before the storm this morning. Turns out a section of the fence was down. He claims my bull did it. I don't believe it, but I promised to round up my stock as soon as the storm cleared. But I can't get to the fence until next week. That's when old Oscar blew up."

"Fence down, cattle loose—is this the kind of thing that's been happening to you?" Frank asked.

Roy nodded, deep frown lines cutting his forehead. "It started with gates left open, fences down—or cut—a phone line out. Then a calf or two began to disappear, and the horses showed up lame. It's hard enough making a living out here. Now I've got someone trying to bleed us dry, a drop at a time."

"So that's why you called Dad?" Frank asked.

Roy frowned. "No, I called him after Rudy went down to the south tank a couple of days ago and found eleven head dead."

"Tank?" Joe asked, looking confused.

"It's like a little lake," Frank told him. He turned to Roy. "You think somebody poisoned them?"

"I'd bet on it," Roy said grimly.

"Poisoned them how?" Joe asked.

"Salt water, that's how."

"Salt water!" the boys exclaimed together.

"Where would anybody get *salt* water around here?" Joe asked. "There's no ocean in a thousand miles."

"Out of an oil well, maybe," Frank suggested.

"You've got to be kidding," Joe said.

"No, Frank's right," Roy cut in. "On some wells, you hit salt water before you hit oil. They pump it out and truck it away. There's a bunch of new wells between here and Armstrong, the county seat. It wouldn't be far for someone to bring a truck full of bad water and dump it into my tank."

His frown deepened. "And the only clue we found was tire tracks—plenty of them, and plenty wide."

Frank nodded. "Like a truck's tires."

Joe changed the subject. "Had Owens seen Jerry?"

"I didn't have a chance to ask. He just yelled and was out of here."

"There were two messages on the answering machine," Frank told him. "From Jerry. The first was a test. The second time he sounded nervous, talking about lights at the old homestead. He was going to take a look."

Roy looked surprised. "This I want to hear," he said, leading the way inside. After he'd heard the message, his look changed to one of worry.

"What's this old homestead?" Joe asked.

"It was the first house in these parts," Roy said. "Not much more than a ruin, now. It just happens to be right on the boundary between Oscar Owens's place and mine."

He went to the window. "Looks like the storm's about over. I've got to wait for the sheriff, but maybe you could check out the homestead for me." He peered at Joe. "Can you handle that beat-up yellow pickup out front? It's got an old three-speed 'tranny.' "

Joe's eyes lit up. "Sure thing!" he exclaimed, catching the key Roy tossed him.

The sky was clearing, and as the boys stepped through the front door they took in their new surroundings. The ranch house was on a ridge facing east. Below, at the bottom of the slope, was a sheet-metal barn and a cluster of buildings—a garage, maintenance shop, and various other sheds. Beyond, to the east, lay a vast stretch of rolling treeless country. The lowlands were covered with shrubs and small bushy trees, broken occasionally by bare, light-colored hills. Against the horizon lay a long, curved line.

"Is that the caprock?" Joe asked.

"You got it," Roy said. He pointed slightly southeast. "The bunkhouse is a couple of miles in that direction, just off the top of the caprock." He glanced at Joe. "That's an easy place to get stuck, if you don't watch yourself."

"Where's the homestead?" Frank asked.

Roy pointed due south, along the ridge.

"That way, about five miles. If you take the road that you came in on, you'll come to a fork. Take the leg that heads south."

Frank was staring at something at the foot of the hill—it looked like a wind sock that airports use. The brush on both sides of a flat stretch of road had been cleared away, but the "runway" was too short to handle an ordinary aircraft. "Is somebody flying an ultralight?" he asked.

Roy gave him an appraising glance. "You know about that new miniplane Jerry's flying?"

"Jerry's got an ultralight?" Joe asked, surprised. "What does he do with it?"

"He runs cattle out of the bush with it," Roy explained. "He read somewhere that they use helicopters for that kind of work down south, and he reckoned that an ultralight would do just as good and be a lot cheaper."

He shrugged. "Thing looks to me about as solid as a butterfly, but he talked me into it. It's easy for him to fly, and he can spot cattle we'd never see from the ground. The thing makes a whale of a racket, so he gets behind the cattle and drives them along like a good cow dog."

"Where is it now?" Frank wanted to know.

"Down in the barn." Roy looked at them. "Either of you boys fly?"

"I'm learning," Frank said. "Can I have a look at it?"

Roy nodded. "It sure could speed up the search."

"But you only just got your *student's* license," Joe objected quietly so only Frank could hear.

Frank was already heading down the hill. "Doesn't matter," he said out of the side of his mouth. "Federal regulations don't require a license for flying an ultralight, as long as it's under a certain weight and flies less than fifty miles an hour—and as long as there are no passengers."

In the dim light inside the barn, Frank whistled softly, "She's a beauty, Roy."

The ultralight had long, red, heavy nylon wings with yellow stripes. The aluminum tubes that supported the wings and connected them to the tail and the tricycle undercarriage were also red. The engine was hung under the rear edge of the wing, and the prop stuck out behind it. There were two bucket seats over the wheels.

"These look like the controls on the trainer I fly," Frank remarked, climbing in from the left. "But it's a lot more open."

Joe grinned. "Sort of like a motorcycle of airplanes."

"This would sure help a lot in searching for Jerry." Frank looked at Roy. "Mind if we wheel it outside and try it?"

"If you think you can handle it," Roy said.

A minute later Frank was sitting inches above the dirt road, facing into the wind. The engine whined like a chain saw. He tried the hand controls to check the movement of the ailerons. "If I did this in the air, it would make the wings waggle left to right."

Then he checked the elevators on the tail. "This would make the tail go up or down." Finally, Frank worked the foot controls side to side as the rudder on the tail moved back and forth.

"Let me guess," Joe yelled over the noise of the engine as he steadied the right wing. "This is for right or left turns?"

Frank nodded and gave a thumbs-up to Joe. "I'll just take off, circle, and land," he shouted, and pulled back the throttle.

The ultralight seemed to spring forward. Frank felt the blast of the air rushing past him as he rose. Soon he was even with the ranch house at the top of the hill, at an altitude of a hundred feet or so, and he began his turn to the left, still climbing.

As he passed over the ranch house, he reduced power and began to glide, continuing his turn. The road was now directly in front of him and a little below. He leveled the wings and eased back on the elevator, slowing his descent and reducing his speed. He was sailing between the scrub on both sides of the road when he felt the wheels bounce. Carefully, he applied the brake and came to a smooth stop.

"How was it?" Roy shouted, as Frank cut the engine.

"Great!" Frank replied. "It works fine."

"So what's our next move?" Joe asked.

"You take the truck and head for the homestead. I'll shadow you from the air."

"How do we communicate?" Joe asked doubtfully. "That thing doesn't have a radio."

"Arm and hand signals, I guess. If I spot something, I'll circle and point at it."

"Good luck," Roy said.

Joe climbed into the yellow pickup. From the looks of it, the truck had lived its whole life on the ranch and had never seen a car wash or a vacuum cleaner. He turned the key and its giant V-8 engine thundered to life. He grinned. The muffler had seen better days, but maybe the cows didn't mind. He pulled down on the massive stick shift. There was an angry grating sound.

Transmission could use some work, he thought. Joe shoved into first gear, and the truck lurched off. He turned down the hill just in time to see Frank making his takeoff run.

The road forked half a mile to the north. Joe twisted the wheel to the left and headed south, down a road with plenty of washouts. Frank was hovering off to one side, at an altitude of about a hundred feet. He could easily outdistance the truck, but he was holding back.

The sun was low in the west. All at once Frank took the lead, circling about a hundred yards ahead. Joe was almost on top of the homestead before he saw it through the ferny fronds of six-foot-high mesquite bushes.

It was a single-room shack, weather-beaten and sagging. Behind it was a corral and loading pens. A few small trees had grown up around the abandoned wooden windmill.

If there had been any tracks in the sand, the wind had erased them. He stopped the truck, left it running, and opened the door to the shack. Inside was a bunk in one corner and a table in the middle, with a couple of wooden chairs. Papers, bottles, and cans lay on the cracked cement floor, around an old iron stove. But there was no sign of life—not even a footprint in the fine layer of grit that covered everything.

When Joe stepped outside, he saw Frank high above, heading east. He jumped into the truck and gunned it into pursuit.

Up in the ultralight, Frank had seen something moving up ahead, among the sand hills. He had soared over to check it out while Joe searched the house. As Frank flew closer he saw it was a horse—a horse with a saddle but no rider. It could be the horse Jerry had been riding when he went to check out the lights.

He banked, preparing to circle back to the homestead. Suddenly he felt a jerk on his right foot pedal, the one that controlled the right rudder. Then the ultralight whipped into a spin.

Frank frantically worked the rudder pedals. The right one was stuck in the stop position. Trying the left pedal, he managed to move it slightly—but then it stuck, too.

Fighting panic, Frank glanced behind him at the tail. The rudder was definitely jammed, which meant that a control cable must have broken and the control line had fouled.

The ultralight kept whirling in a tight circle—and the ground was moving up closer and closer.

If Frank didn't get control back, the ultralight would crash!

Chapter 3

STAY COOL! That was what Frank's flight instructor always said. The foot controls didn't work, but what about the hand controls? Gingerly Frank tried the control stick. The ultralight banked to the right, stopping its spin.

"All *right!*" Frank muttered. "I've still got the aileron controls and can make wide turns. But I'll be flying with crossed controls—if I don't watch it, I'll either stall out or wind up in another spin. Either way, I'll fall—and there's nowhere safe to land right here."

Using the stick, Frank carefully fought the spin to bring the ultralight shakily around. Then he leveled it out at about a hundred feet. He was heading back for the ranch when he saw Joe's yellow truck on the road below. Joe, his head out the window, was staring up at him.

Got to let Joe know what's wrong, Frank thought. He pointed to the ultralight's tail and shook his head violently. He pointed to himself, then toward the ranch. Then he pointed down at the truck and toward the sand hills where he'd seen the horse.

Joe stopped the truck and climbed out, looking up. Frank repeated the gestures. This time, Joe gave him a thumbs-up sign, got back in the truck, and started off.

Frank had a long, nervous flight back to the ranch. He still wasn't home free—landing with crossed controls would be tricky. But he'd practiced cross-wind landings, which also made planes spin. The trick was to kick in the rudder at the last possible moment to make the plane straighten out. But Frank had no rudder!

He reduced power as much as he dared, slowly bringing the ultralight's nose up. He was coming straight down the road, aiming slightly to the left, his right wing a little low. Just before touchdown, he jammed all his weight on the right brake. The ultralight landed on the right wheel, bounced, pulled violently to the right, then straightened out.

Roy ran up to the plane. "Where'd you learn to fly like that?" he asked.

Frank managed a shaky breath. "Just lucky?" he said.

* * *

Joe knew something was wrong, but he didn't know what. His first instinct was to follow Frank, in case he was in real trouble. But Frank had obviously spotted something he wanted Joe to check out. So Joe continued toward the sand hills.

When he got to the edge of the low dunes, the road narrowed to a trail and then disappeared altogether. Joe remembered what Roy had said about getting stuck, so he stopped the truck, climbed out, and started to climb the nearest dune for a look. There wasn't much vegetation, and it was slow going in the loose sand.

As he reached the top of the dune, the sun was dipping below the horizon. Twenty yards away, Joe saw what Frank must have spotted from the air—a riderless bay horse, reins trailing in the sand.

Joe approached cautiously, afraid the horse would bolt. But the animal was exhausted. It just stood with its head down as Joe grabbed the reins. "Hey, fella, where's your rider?"

Joe led the horse to the truck, tied it to a bush so it could graze the tall grass, then headed back up the hill. Trailing the hoofprints brought him to a small hollow—the horse must have taken shelter there during the storm. Joe saw no trace of the rider.

He headed back to the truck and sat down

on the tailgate to watch the gathering shadows. "Hope Frank comes back quick with reinforcements."

Finally two sets of headlights appeared from the darkness. The lead truck slid to a stop and Frank jumped out. Roy pulled in behind, towing a horse trailer. A small, wiry man with dark, straight hair and a broad, flat face got out with him as a gray dog leaped from the truck bed and trotted toward the horse, whining.

"Glad you could make it." Joe grinned at Frank. "How come you cut out back there?"

"The rudder cable broke," Frank replied. "It was some trick getting down in one piece."

"But he did it—good job, too," Roy said. He looked at the horse. "That's Jerry's bay, all right. Where'd you find him?"

"Over there," Joe said, pointing. "I didn't find anything else—no tracks."

"Rudy, take Shep and have a look," Roy told the other man. "We'll load the horse."

"Shep! *Venga!*" Rudy commanded. The dog whined and sat down beside the horse. "Come here!" Reluctantly, the dog got up and trotted after him.

"That's Rudy Castillo," Roy told Joe, pulling down the trailer tailgate. "Fine ranch hand. He's got a sixth sense—if there's anything out there, he'll spot it."

"And the dog?" Frank asked as they loaded the horse.

"Shep belongs to Jerry." Roy shook his head and frowned. "That was one funny thing I noticed at the bunkhouse—Shep wasn't there. Rudy said he showed up a little while ago. There was something else—"

Rudy came up, shaking his head. "No sign of him, Senor Roy."

Roy nodded grimly. "Well, I guess that's it for now. Let's head back to the ranch. I called the sheriff and told him to come later. I don't want to miss him. We can get some supper, too. They piled into the trucks and headed back.

"That was delicious," Joe told Dot as he polished off the biggest meal of chicken-fried steak he'd ever eaten. "If supper's always like this, I may sign on permanently." Everyone laughed.

"I want to hear more about the grazing leases you told me about earlier," Frank said to Roy. "You're renting some land? You don't own all fifty thousand acres?"

"Right," Roy said, pushing his chair back. He led them into the office and pointed at a large wall map, a section of which was outlined in red. "We actually own this part." His hand moved along the middle third of the outlined area. "This is state land." He traced out a section to the north. "We lease the south end of the ranch—the sand hills section—from the federal government. In fact, our leases are up for renewal next month."

"So you get to use the land?" Joe asked.

Roy grinned. "We get to use the grass on it to feed our stock. And we get the right to renew it. The leases are so cheap that nobody ever lets them go unrenewed."

A car pulled up outside, then came a knock at the front door. "Hi, Bobby," they heard Dot say. "Roy's in the office."

A man in a dusty khaki uniform stepped in the room. The sheriff was slender and just over thirty. He wore a badge, and a .357 Magnum was holstered at his hip. "Evening, Roy. Jerry show up yet?"

"Not yet," Roy said. "Boys, this is Bobby Clinton, our local sheriff. Bobby, this is Frank and Joe Hardy. I worked with their father awhile back. They're here to help me straighten out those problems I've been having."

The sheriff nodded. "Welcome to Armstrong County." His eyes weren't welcoming, however, as he gave Frank and Joe the once-over. Clinton turned back to Roy. "You want me to file a missing persons report on Jerry, or do you want to wait a few days to see if he wanders in?"

"We found his horse this afternoon, out in the sand hills," Joe volunteered.

The sheriff gave him a thin smile. "He must

have got bucked off,'' he said. ''Chances are he'll come walking in tomorrow morning, complaining about sore feet.''

Roy fixed his eyes on the sheriff and shook his head. ''You don't believe that. I think Jerry was riding before he could walk.''

''Well, what then?''

''I don't know,'' Roy said slowly. ''We're going looking in the morning.''

''Guess I could spare a couple of deputies,'' the sheriff offered. ''And I'll talk to a few of the other ranchers.''

Roy nodded. ''Have them meet us by the bunkhouse up on the caprock at sunup.''

Clinton left, and Roy turned to Frank and Joe, grinning crookedly. ''Bobby's what we call 'a good ol' boy.' Problem is, he's still got a lot to learn about being a good sheriff.''

''Maybe there's a connection between Jerry's disappearance and the other problems,'' Joe said.

''I don't know,'' Roy said. ''But I'll tell you one thing. Remember when we picked you up, I said something was funny. I just figured out what it is. Why would Jerry ride his horse from the bunkhouse to the old homestead at night, in the dark? He would've used the truck. But he didn't—it was still there.''

''So somebody went to a lot of trouble to make us *think* Jerry took the horse,'' Frank suggested.

"Maybe," Roy agreed, with a frown. "That doesn't sound good."

"Would Jerry—or you—have an enemy who'd want to get rid of him?" Joe asked.

For a moment Roy was silent. Then he said, "Jerry didn't, but I might."

"Can you give us some names?" Frank said.

Roy's voice was reluctant. "I don't like to bad-mouth a man without proof."

"We understand," Frank said. "But we've got to have some leads."

"Well, the first name that comes to mind is Jake Grimes," Roy said. "He was a hand here last year, but I had to let him go because I caught him selling off some of the ranch supplies." He grunted. "He and Jerry parted on good terms, but Jake was pretty angry with me."

"Where can we find him?" Frank asked.

"He was working in Armstrong, last I heard. For the feed lot."

"What about Oscar Owens?" Joe asked. "He didn't sound like your best buddy when he left here this afternoon."

"Oh, Oscar yells a lot," Roy admitted, "but it doesn't usually amount to anything." He straightened his shoulders. "But for right now, let's concentrate on finding Jerry. I don't think he's wandering around out there. But if he is, he won't last more than another day in this heat, without water."

"What about the ultralight?" Joe asked Frank. "Can it be repaired to help with the search?"

Frank shook his head. "I checked it out. It needs a new rudder cable."

"Not enough time for that," Roy told them. "Tomorrow we'll drive into the back country. It's easy to get lost if you don't know your way, so one of you can come with me, the other will go with Rudy."

Frank and Joe agreed.

At dawn the next day a dozen trucks and jeeps were parked at the bunkhouse, a small neat building just off the road along the top of the caprock. There were the usual barns and corrals, and out back, beside a propane tank, there was a satellite dish.

"Can we have a look inside?" Frank asked Roy.

Roy unlocked the front door. "Go ahead. But you'd better hurry. We'll get started as soon as Bobby Clinton's boys show up."

The bunkhouse had apparently once been a rancher's main home. Now, though, it looked more like a bachelor pad. In the bedroom there were posters of several appealing young movie stars, a gun rack on the wall, and a closet full of cowboy boots, work shirts, and blue jeans.

The living room was nearly bare, except for a TV and a stereo, with a rack of country and western cassettes. There was a half-eaten pizza on the kitchen counter beside the microwave. As far as clues were concerned, nothing.

Outside, Roy was talking to the group—about thirty men, including a couple of uniformed deputies who had just arrived. "Okay, boys. You all know that Jerry disappeared night before last. We found his horse yesterday afternoon, near the old homestead. So that cuts down the area we've got to search."

"Great," Joe overheard one of the searchers whisper to another. "That cuts us down to about twenty square miles of desert."

Roy broke the group up into pairs and assigned them search areas. In a few minutes everyone climbed into vehicles.

Frank rode with Roy in a green pickup with a CB radio. All morning they bounced up one rutted road and down another, leaving a trail of dust. At each windmill or water tank, Roy stopped and got on the radio while Frank pushed through a cluster of cows and climbed the tower. He then scanned the area with a pair of powerful binoculars. Actually, he was glad that he and Joe weren't out on their own. Every road, every windmill, every tank, looked exactly alike.

For lunch they headed back to the ranch house. Frank and Joe were surprised that Nat Wilkin was there, along with a couple of other searchers.

"Any news?" Roy asked.

Nat shook his head. "Sorry, Roy, all the groups reported the same thing—no luck."

They ate quickly, then headed out for another bone-jarring tour of dusty scenery. Just before sundown, the searchers met back at the ranch house again. They all looked dejected.

"Nothing," Nat said. "I'm available tomorrow, if you want—"

Roy shook his head. "Thanks for the help, boys." The searchers left in silence.

"They're not coming back tomorrow?" Joe asked.

Roy shook his head wearily. "No point. We covered the territory pretty thoroughly. If Jerry's out there alive, which I doubt, his only hope is to get to one of those water tanks. Rudy and I'll keep checking them out."

Frank nodded. "Joe and I would like to camp out at the old homestead," he said. "If Jerry really saw something suspicious down there, we want to know what it is."

"That's as good an idea as any," Roy said. "Dot will make you some sandwiches. Load a couple of mattresses into the green pickup, the one with the CB. That way, you can keep in touch."

It was dark by the time Frank and Joe finally made it to the old shack. Their lantern lit the single room, casting shadows into the corners. Outside, the wind moaned in the mesquite trees. Then the boys heard the sound of twigs breaking underfoot.

Joe grinned. "You think there are bears in this country?"

"I doubt it," Frank said in a low voice. "And we didn't hear an engine. Let's check this out."

The Hardys rose to their feet and headed silently for the door.

Just as silently, someone outside was lifting the rusty old latch on the door.

Chapter 4

The door opened a crack. Frank and Joe froze in their tracks as something was thrust through the door. It looked like an old gourd on a stick. An ancient hand then appeared, clutching the stick and shaking it. The gourd rattled.

Then the door creaked open all the way, to reveal an old man with stringy gray hair. He wore a straw sombrero and carried a straw bag.

"It's him!" Joe whispered excitedly. "Caprock Charlie—the old man I saw in the dust storm!"

"Hello," Frank said, nodding to their uninvited guest.

"*Buenas noches*." The old man looked at both boys, rattling the gourd again. "Call me Carlos. I come with a warning."

"Warning?" Joe asked. "About what?"

"There is evil here," the old man whispered. "Danger." He pointed out the window to the east. "You see?"

Joe turned to see a crescent moon rising over the caprock. "That's weird," he muttered. "I've never seen a ring around the moon like that."

Frank shrugged it off scientifically. "Ice crystals at high altitudes," he said.

The old man stepped forward to draw a *C* in the dust on the table with his finger. Around the *C* he drew a circle. *"Muy malo!"* he exclaimed. "Very bad."

"That's Roy's brand," Joe said in a low voice.

"It's also the crescent moon," Frank pointed out, "with a ring around it." He turned to the old man. "What does it mean?"

"Long ago," the old man said, "comancheros attacked settlers who came to live up there." He pointed to the caprock. "Near my people's sacred place. All the settlers but one died that night, when the moon was a ringed crescent, like now. You must leave and not come back!"

Outside, a cow bellowed. The sound distracted the Hardys, who turned to the window. As they turned back, they felt a swift, chill breeze. The room was empty.

"Let's go after him," Joe said, heading for

the door. But outside, they saw no sign of the old man.

"Forget it, Joe," Frank told him. "That guy's got some vanishing act. If we go after him, they'll be looking for us in the morning."

"Okay," Joe agreed, as they stepped back inside. "What say we get some sleep?"

Joe woke well after midnight, stirring restlessly on his mattress. He'd heard something—no, *felt* something. It was like a clap of thunder, reverberating in his bones. Through the window he could see that the moon had moved far to the west in the cloudless sky. No thunder. He must have been dreaming.

When he awoke again, it was almost daylight. Frank's alarm watch was beeping.

"Give me a break." Joe sighed sleepily.

Frank was heading for the door. "I promised to check in with Roy on the CB at seven. After I do that, maybe we can check out some dead cattle."

After Frank finished on the CB, they set off to find the stock tank. A quarter mile south of the homestead, Joe slowed the truck and pointed to a dozen large black birds circling just ahead. "Buzzards?"

"Vultures, actually," Frank said. "Scavengers. That must be the place."

Just off the road, an earth dam had been pushed up across a dry stream bed. Most of the water in the tank had evaporated, and all that was left was a puddle of green water, thick with pond scum. The edge of the puddle had a thick white crust. Deep tire ruts filled with drifted sand led from the road to the tank.

Joe sniffed. Nearby, at the edge of the sagebrush, were the carcasses of several cattle. "I thought they got rid of the dead cattle. These must have been new customers."

Frank knelt beside the puddle. "Looks like salt, all right," he said. "Why don't you collect a sample of the crust, and fill a bottle with water. I'll have a look around."

While Joe collected the samples, Frank inspected the ruts and then walked around the tank, looking at the ground. Joe saw him pick something up, sniff it, and put it into a plastic bag. "What did you find?"

Frank handed him a plastic bag with three shiny rifle cartridge cases in it. "They're fresh."

"What kind of gun?"

"Can't tell. They've got military ordnance marks on the bottom—number forty-three. Probably the year of manufacture, not the caliber. I'd say they're World War II surplus." He examined them closely. "Weird looking. The base and the shoulder are unusually short, and the base has a lot of taper. I'd guess they're about thirty caliber."

"Maybe Roy or Rudy shot some of the cattle that were too far gone to save," Joe suggested.

"Maybe. We'll ask." Frank looked at the tire tracks. "I don't think there's any point in trying to make casts of the tracks—they're too badly eroded by the wind. But I think our major clue is the tank truck that left them. Let's head for the ranch house. I've got some questions for Roy."

As they drove up to the ranch house, Roy came out to greet them. He shook his head when he saw the cartridges. "We didn't shoot any cattle. But that tank attracts game and people hunt out there all the time."

"We were thinking of trying to find the truck that poisoned the tank. Can you give us some idea about where to look?" Joe asked, as Frank stuck the plastic bag with the cartridges back into the glove compartment.

"You can try the oil-drilling services in Armstrong," Roy said. "Plenty of those companies use trucks like that—probably too many to check out."

"Well, we'll give it a try," Frank said.

They drove to Armstrong, the county seat thirty miles to the southeast. The town was an odd mixture of western cow town and modern city. The outskirts housed companies supplying the relatively new oil and agricultural economy. But in the heart of town, the courthouse was surrounded by old stores that had gone up around the turn of the century.

"Let's start here," Frank said, pulling into

the parking lot of the Acme Drilling Service Company. He parked beside a truck hitched to a huge tank trailer.

"Look at the size of those tires," Joe said, marveling.

"Big enough to fill the ruts at the stock tank," Frank said as they got out.

"Help you boys?" the man behind the counter asked.

"Are you the dispatcher?" Frank asked.

The man grinned. "Among other things."

"We're looking for a tank truck."

"We lease by the hour, the day, or the week. How long you need it?"

"What we need is information," Frank said. "The truck we're looking for was involved in illegal dumping."

"Registration number?" the dispatcher growled.

"We don't know," Frank admitted.

"What makes you think it was our truck?"

"We're just trying to figure out where it could have come from," Frank said. "How many companies lease trucks around here?"

The dispatcher barked a laugh. "At least three others I know of. Plus half a dozen independents."

"Nine companies, just in this town." Frank began to understand what Roy had meant. "Do these trucks keep any kind of a log?" he asked.

"Most don't. We've got better things to do

with our time." The dispatcher scowled. "Like make a living."

"Do you know of any trucks working up near the town of Caprock?" Frank asked.

The dispatcher seemed to relax a little. "Nope. As far as I know, there's no drilling going on there." He eyed them. "What kind of dumping?"

"Uh, nothing, I guess," Frank said, tugging on Joe's arm. "Thanks for your help." They headed for the door.

"That didn't get us anywhere," Joe said grimly as they crossed the lot.

Frank shrugged. "I guess Roy was right. Let's head back to the ranch. Maybe they've heard something from Jerry."

The sky had been clear all day, but as they drove north, threatening gray clouds began to loom against the horizon, dark and heavy. Bright lightning flickered in all directions.

"Looks like we get to see one of those famous desert thunderstorms," Frank said.

As they drove into the approaching storm, the black clouds seemed to rise like a dark curtain, then lower behind them until the horizon at their backs was only a narrow, eerie strip of pale light. No wind stirred the oppressive layer of heat that blanketed the desert, but overhead the clouds were boiling and the black had turned to a peculiar violet-green.

"I don't like the looks of this," Joe muttered, pointing at a dark mass hanging below the cloud base.

Suddenly, less than a quarter-mile away, a long, dark finger reached out of the blackness and groped toward the ground.

It touched down, bounced up, then came back down beside a roadside sign. Joe stared as the billboard disintegrated, sucked up into the darkness.

"Did you see *that?*" Frank gasped, pulling onto the shoulder and stopping.

The tornado lifted up again, pulling a stream of dirt and dust after it. Then, with the roar of an immense freight train, the twister came directly at them!

Chapter 5

"QUICK! INTO THE DITCH!" Joe heard Frank shout, over the deafening roar.

It was so black that Joe could barely see the edge of the road as he jumped out of the truck and flung himself into the shallow ditch. He kept himself flattened against the ground as the wind worked hard to pry him loose. Minutes ticked by as the storm roared around them, the air thick with dirt and gravel and twisted shrubs. Finally the noise died down.

"You okay?" Frank asked, behind Joe.

"Yeah." Joe sat up, rubbing his shoulder. "Hey! Where's the truck?"

Frank was on his knees, looking a little gray. "I think that's it," he said, pointing. In a field several hundred feet away was a mass of crumpled metal.

"Guess we can chalk up one truck to the storm," Joe grunted, getting to his feet. He shivered. The air, which had been like a blast from an oven only minutes before, now felt refrigerated. The storm had dropped the temperature at least forty degrees in just minutes. A few chilly drops of rain began to fall.

"Come on. Let's take a look," Frank said.

The truck lay on the driver's side. The top had caved in, with the passenger door wrenched off. The glove compartment was open and empty. Five minutes of searching didn't turn up the bag of cartridges.

"So much for our evidence," Joe sighed. "Think you'd recognize those cartridges if you saw them again?"

Frank nodded. "They were pretty unusual."

Joe took a last look at the truck. It was beginning to rain heavily now. "This thing's not going anywhere," he said. "Let's head back to the road. Maybe we can hitch a ride."

They had scarcely reached the road when they saw the flashing lights of an emergency vehicle approaching at high speed. The car—a highway patrol car—slowed as it neared them. The trooper pulled onto the shoulder and rolled down his passenger window.

"The weather service just put out a tornado bulletin. You guys better be on the lookout."

Joe laughed. "We've already seen as much of that tornado as we care to." He jerked his thumb over his shoulder. "It totaled our truck."

The trooper glanced toward the wreckage and let out a whistle of surprise. "Anybody hurt?"

Frank shook his head. "Nope. We hit the dirt just in time."

The trooper opened the door. "Come on in—you're getting wet."

The boys listened while the trooper got on the radio and made a report. When he finished, he turned to them. "Which way you headed?"

"North," Joe said. "To town—Caprock."

"That's my patrol," the trooper said. "I'll give you a ride."

The trooper eased the patrol car back onto the highway. After a while, he asked, "You guys from around here?"

"We're visiting Roy Carlson, on the Circle C," Frank replied.

"I picked up a missing persons report about a Circle C hand," the trooper told them. "Has he turned up yet?"

Joe shook his head. "Not yet," he said.

"Well, it's not surprising," the trooper told them. "Young guys pack up and leave all the time, most of them without notice. He'll show up somewhere, sooner or later."

"There's been some trouble out at the ranch—vandalism," Joe said. "Do you see much of that around here?"

The trooper looked surprised. "Not much," he said. "It's too far from town for the punks to come out."

Twenty minutes later the patrol car pulled up in front of the Caprock store. The Hardys thanked the trooper for the ride and climbed out.

"I'll call the ranch." Frank headed for the pay phone. "Somebody can come and pick us up."

"Good idea," Joe said, on his way into the store. "I need something to drink. How about you?"

"Sounds good," Frank replied, dialing the phone.

The inside of the old store was just what Joe had expected. A dusty front window was the only source of light for the small room. The walls were lined with homemade shelves of boards and plywood. Stacked on them were cans and boxes, their labels faded and peeling, and lots of miscellaneous hardware.

To the right of the door was a long wooden counter with a postage scale on it. Behind the counter stood a bank of boxes with numbered glass doors—Caprock's post office. In one corner stood an ancient soda machine filled with bottles. Joe fed it some coins, took out two bottles, and opened them.

"Roy's on his way," Frank said, coming into the store. He took the bottle Joe handed him.

"You boys the ones staying at the Carlson place?"

The question came from the frail, white-haired man behind the counter. Joe had felt his gaze since they walked into the store. Not too many people get dropped off here by the state cops, Joe thought, amused. "Yeah, we lost our truck in a tornado," he said. "The trooper gave us a ride."

The little man's eyebrows shot up. "I'd say you boys are born lucky," he said.

"We hope so," Frank said. "Say, do you know an old Native American guy who hangs out around here? He's got gray hair. I think he carries a straw bag."

"Oh, Charlie. Sure, I know him. He was here when I came and that's been—well, let's see." He calculated. "Better than forty years now."

"Where does he live?" Frank asked.

The white-haired man shifted uneasily. "Here and there. Mostly in a shack below the caprock. How come you want to know?"

"We've been staying at the old homestead on the edge of the sand hills," Joe replied. "He paid us a visit last night with a crazy story about a Native American raid under a crescent moon with a halo around it."

"Yep, that sounds like Charlie." The frail man got serious. "But that's no crazy story. About a hundred years ago, a bunch of renegades hit a homesteader's cabin out on the caprock one night. Killed every last soul they could find. Then they burned the place to the ground."

"Charlie said they were comancheros," Frank interrupted. "And the comancheros weren't all Native Americans, as I understand it. Some of them were Mexicans, others were renegade whites."

The little man shrugged. "Who cares nowadays? Only one person survived—and he died years ago."

"Charlie was talking about evil and danger," Joe told him. "Do you know what he meant?"

Now the storekeeper laughed. "I wouldn't worry if I were you. Charlie's always trying to scare folks with talk about evil." He grinned, showing one gold tooth. "I think he hopes we'll all get scared, pack up and leave. Then his people can come back to their sacred place."

"Sacred place?" Frank asked curiously. "Charlie mentioned that, too. What tribe does he belong to?"

The old man looked doubtful. "I really don't know—Kiowa, maybe. I've heard that their sacred place was near where they killed those settlers."

A truck stopped outside and Roy came in. "Afternoon, Matt," he said to the little man. "Hey, you guys okay?" he asked, frowning at the Hardys.

"We're fine," Frank assured him. "Sorry about the truck, though. There's not much left." He turned to the little man. "Thanks for the information."

"Don't mention it," Matt said.

On the way back to the ranch, the brothers described their narrow escape from the tornado, and then filled Roy in on their lack of success in Armstrong. As it turned out, Roy and Rudy hadn't been successful either. They had patrolled the tanks all day without finding a single sign of Jerry.

"We'll spend the night at the homestead," Frank said, as they neared the ranch house. "Maybe Charlie will pay us another visit."

Roy nodded. "Might be good if you could talk to him."

"Why? You don't think he's got anything to do with what's happened, do you?" Joe asked.

"Not directly," Roy replied, hesitating. "But there's not much that goes on around here that he doesn't know about. No telling what he's seen. He might just solve the whole riddle on the spot, if he's got a mind to it."

After dinner Frank and Joe returned to the homestead. The wind had picked up and there was a chill in the desert night.

"What say we try out that old iron stove?" Joe asked. Dot had made them a thermos of breakfast coffee, and he set it on the table.

Frank set up the lantern. "Charlie will see

our light—so we don't have to worry about smoke signals."

Joe lifted one of the heavy, round stove covers. "Looks like somebody left this thing full of kindling," he said. "Did Roy give you any matches?"

Frank tossed over a pack of matches. Joe struck one, touched it to a piece of paper under the pile of wood splinters in the stove, and watched the flame grow. "That's funny," he said.

"What's that?" Frank asked, coming to stand beside him.

"This stuff is hissing like green wood—but it's burning fine. Not even any smoke."

Frank poked the kindling with a lid handle. It shifted slightly, to reveal what looked like a short length of heavy cord, sizzling hotly.

Frank jumped back. "That's a blasting fuse!" he yelled. "They use it to set off dynamite!"

Chapter 6

"LET'S DOUSE IT." Joe grabbed for the thermos of coffee on the table.

"Are you nuts?" Frank jerked his arm and towed him toward the door. "Run!" Joe sprinted through the yard just behind his brother. As he dove for cover behind a metal horse trough, a hot blast caught him from behind. Then he was sailing through the air.

A moment later Frank was shaking his shoulder. "Joe! Joe, are you all right?"

Joe opened his eyes. He lay facedown beside Frank, his mouth full of dust, his ears ringing. His right shoulder felt as if it had been hit by a sledgehammer when he struggled to sit up. Splintered cedar shingles fluttered down out of the night sky like a flock of wooden butterflies. Joe shook his head and began to laugh.

"What's so funny?" Frank demanded in a low voice, irritated.

"Oh, nothing." Joe gritted his teeth. Laughing hurt his shoulder and his chest. "I guess it's just good to be alive."

"You're right about that," Frank whispered. "But we'd better lie low, just in case whoever rigged that little surprise is still hanging around to check out the damage."

"They couldn't have done a better job on that cabin with an artillery strike," Joe whispered back. In the moonlight he could see that there was nothing left of the cabin. The walls and floor were scattered around the yard.

"We're lucky we didn't catch any cast iron from that stove," Frank said. "That blast must have sent pieces flying like shrapnel. Whoever's behind this just graduated from dirty tricks and suspected kidnapping to attempted murder."

"At least the blast blew out the fire," Joe said. "It would have been a real mess if it had started a brush fire, dry as it is around here."

They lay in silence as the crescent moon climbed over the caprock. The wind-blown mesquite branches painted moving shadows across the rough landscape, fooling the Hardys' eyes.

Finally Frank decided to get a reaction from anyone skulking around. He picked up a rock, tossing it at the old storage tank beside the abandoned windmill. The tank gave off a hollow boom, but that was the only sound they heard.

"Looks clear," Frank whispered. "Let's work our way to the truck and get out of here."

Joe slithered forward, trying to ignore the pain in his shoulder. "And what if they booby-trapped *that*, too?" he wanted to know.

Frank grinned. "Are you trying to spoil my night?"

"Just being cautious," Joe retorted. "If I had checked out the stove first—"

"Don't worry. We'll look before we drive."

They crawled on their bellies to the pickup. Still keeping low, they checked over the wheels, behind the seat, and finally in the engine compartment.

"Looks clear to me," Joe said at last. "I'm ready to chance it. You?"

Frank nodded. "I guess. I sure don't want to hang out here until dawn. Think you can make it to the road without any lights?" He climbed into the truck.

"Watch me." Joe slipped into the driver's seat, put the key into the ignition, and with a deep breath, turned it.

The engine roared to life. In a split second Joe had shifted the truck into low, and it was bouncing from rock to rock between the mesquite toward the road.

"Okay," Frank said as Joe expertly whipped

the truck over the ditch and onto the dirt road. "Let there be light!"

Joe switched on the high beams. On the quick trip back to the ranch house, they saw no sign of life except for one startled antelope that bounded across the road in front of them.

When they arrived, Jerry's dog greeted them with a wild flurry of barking. By the time Joe switched off the engine, lights were coming on all over the house.

Roy stuck his head out the front door. "Trouble, boys?"

"Just a little rural renewal." Joe's voice was tight. "Somebody blew up the old homestead."

After Roy had heard their story, he said, "You should be safe enough here tonight. Nobody's going to set foot on this place without Shep letting us know about it."

Frank climbed out of the truck. "I think we could use a safe night's sleep. But first thing in the morning," he added with determination, "we're heading for Armstrong. I think it's time we looked for a replacement cable for the ultralight. And we're going to look up that former hand of yours—Jake Grimes. I wonder if he's been playing with dynamite lately."

Joe's shoulder was a little stiff the next morning, but aside from that, the boys were none the worse for their narrow escape. It was late morning before they were on their way to Armstrong. They drove past the spot where the tornado had slammed their truck off the road.

"Roy said he called the insurance company," Joe commented. "After they take a look at it, it'll get hauled off for salvage."

On the outskirts of Armstrong, they stopped to get Grimes's address out of the phone book. The place they were looking for was a rundown house a couple of blocks off the square.

"Grimes might be at work," Frank said, as they pulled up out front. "If he is, we'll try the neighbors—find out what they know about the guy."

An angry snarl greeted their knock. "What?"

"Mr. Grimes?" Frank said, to the closed door.

"Bug off! I can't pay you—I'm flat broke."

"We're not bill collectors," Frank said in his most sympathetic voice. "We need your help."

"Help, huh?" Now the voice was suspicious. "I wish somebody would help *me*." There was a grunt, then a noise like somebody dragging a heavy weight. "Hang on."

In a moment the door opened slowly and the boys were greeted by a scowling, round-bellied man in need of a shave. He had a crutch under each arm and his right pants leg was ripped to reveal a heavy plaster cast from his ankle to the top of his thigh. "Well? Say your business and be quick about it."

Frank exchanged glances with Joe. Obviously, Jake Grimes wasn't in any shape to go prowling around old cabins, setting dynamite charges.

"We understand that you used to work on the Circle C," Frank said a little hesitantly.

"What if I did?" Grimes growled.

"There's been trouble out there," Joe said. "We need some information."

Grimes slammed the door in their faces. "Well, you won't get it out of me," he screamed.

"Jerry Greene's disappeared," Frank called through the door on a hunch. Roy had said that Grimes parted on good terms with Jerry. They might have been friends.

There was a silence. Then the door opened a crack. "What's that about Jerry?"

"He disappeared two nights ago," Frank said.

The door swung open. "Come on in," Grimes said. He led the way into a tiny living room, littered with beer cans and old newspapers, and dropped down into a ratty-looking overstuffed chair. "I don't have much use for old man Carlson, but that kid was okay."

Frank glanced at the cast. "When did you hurt your leg?" he asked casually.

"Last week. Got caught between a fence and

a steer with a grudge. Looks like I'll be out of commission for a while." He frowned. "When did Jerry disappear?"

"Sunday night," Frank told him. "As far as we can tell, he went out to check some lights at the old homestead and didn't come back. We're wondering if there was any connection between his disappearance and the dead cattle—and the other things that have happened out there." He eyed Grimes. "You know about the cattle?"

"Heard about it. Bad news, if you ask me, people going around wasting good steers." He grinned bleakly. "I guess somebody else doesn't have any use for Carlson."

"Any idea who?" Joe asked.

Grimes thought for a minute, scratching his stubbly chin. "Nope. None I'd care to name, anyway. How about that old Native American?" He grinned again. "People say he can do magic. Maybe he turned that water to salt."

"What did you think about Grimes?" Frank asked Joe as they sat in a dark corner of a little Mexican restaurant where they'd stopped for something to eat.

"My gut reaction is to cross him off the list," Joe replied, taking a bite of his fajita, a soft tortilla wrapped around spicy slices of beef. "He didn't pretend to hide how he feels about

Roy—and he probably would have if he'd been involved in any of this."

"Yeah," Frank agreed. "With that leg, he'd need an accomplice. My feeling is that he doesn't have the money to hire one. And I'd bet he doesn't have any friends who'd be willing to go out on a limb with him just for the fun of it."

"Uh-huh," Joe replied vaguely. He was looking over Frank's shoulder.

Frank turned to see what Joe was staring at. He grinned. Might have known—a girl. She was slim and attractive, about their age. She wore jeans and hiking boots, and her long dark hair swung down almost to her western belt. Judging from her tanned face and the easy way she moved, she was the outdoor type.

"Hi, Barb," the manager called from behind the counter. "Where've you been lately?"

"Hey, Tony," Barb replied, giving him a smile. *"Cómo está?"* She sat down at the counter and took the mug of coffee that the manager pushed at her. "I've been up in the sand hills collecting samples."

Abruptly Joe got up and went over to the counter. "Pardon me," he said, with his most engaging smile. "I heard you say you'd been up in the sand hills. Was that near Caprock?"

She turned. "That's right. Not far from there." Frank could see that she was giving Joe a suspicious who-wants-to-know look.

"I'm Joe Hardy," Joe said. He turned and pointed to the table. "That's my brother Frank. We're staying at the Circle C, doing a study of our own—kind of." He smiled again. "Maybe you could help us."

Barb regarded him for a minute, the suspicious look turning to an amused glint in her dark eyes. Then she stood up and picked up her coffee mug. "You must be the new guys who've been wandering around town asking questions and tangling with tornadoes."

Joe nodded. "That's us."

"I'm Barbara Harris." The girl shook Joe's hand, then stepped over to the table to shake with Frank.

"How'd you figure out who we were?" Frank asked.

Barbara sat down, flicking her long hair back over her shoulders. "You *are* new," she said with a smile. "And green, too. Don't you know that gossip travels with the speed of light in a small town like this one?" She put her coffee mug down, her smile fading. "Any word about Jerry?"

Joe shook his head. "Nothing."

"You know Jerry?" Frank asked.

"Sure. We went to high school together," Barbara said. "He stayed on at the Circle C, and I enrolled at Eastern New Mexico U." She shrugged. "I'm majoring in geology, with a minor in anthropology."

Barbara grinned. "I was always interested in the Native Americans around here. Anyway, it was a good combination. It got me a great summer job with the BLM, doing a groundwater survey."

"The BLM?" Frank asked.

"Bureau of Land Management." She eyed them. "You know—the guys who handle all the federal land around here."

For the next half hour the boys listened to Barbara talk. She obviously had a detailed knowledge of the area around the Circle C—and not just the physical territory, either. She knew about its history, as well, and all the current events of the entire county.

"Speaking of current events, I see there's a dance in town tomorrow night," Joe said, pointing to the poster on the wall. It announced a dance at the rodeo on Friday.

"I hope you'll be going," Barbara said with a laugh. "We could use some extra males around here, and I could use a date."

"You've got one," Joe said.

"You know, I don't believe you." Frank shook his head as he and Joe left the restaurant.

"How's that?" Joe asked.

"You know what I mean," Frank said, giving him a sharp poke in the ribs. "You find the best-looking girl in town, who turns out to be one of the best informants we've found. And you get invited to dance, as well."

"Just natural talent, I guess," Joe said with a grin, as they reached the pickup. He went to the driver's side, while Frank went to the other.

Joe reached for the door handle. "Funny. I don't remember leaving the window down."

"Joe," Frank commanded. "Get your hand off that door! It's booby-trapped."

Joe dropped his hand and peered inside. He saw a thin yellow wire leading from the door handle on his side to a large paper bag under the steering wheel. "A bomb in a bag," Joe muttered.

"I'll get in and defuse it." The muscles in Frank's arm tensed as his hand tightened on his door handle.

That's when Joe noticed there were *two* wires—the other one led to the handle on Frank's side. If he opened the door, *Frank* would set off the bomb!

Chapter 7

"FRANK—DON'T!" Joe nearly leaped across the hood to keep his brother from opening the door. Frank sucked in a deep breath and joined Joe on the driver's side.

"I didn't figure they'd *double* booby-trap it," he muttered.

"Looks like they didn't care which door was opened—as long as it would blow us both away."

Frank stuck his head and shoulders through the open window, careful not to touch the frame. In the crevice between the door and the seat was a half-sprung rat trap, with a wire connected to the cross bar and another to the base. If Joe had opened the door, the cross bar would have snapped shut onto the base, and the two wires would have made contact.

"A simple but effective firing switch," Frank said. On the seat he spotted a couple of squares of discarded cardboard. "That's what the bomber used to keep the contacts open," he realized, picking them up.

"If you'll take about twenty giant steps back," Frank told Joe, "I'll disarm this monster."

He glanced back to see that Joe was safely behind cover, took a deep breath, and firmly grasped the trap. As he slowly let the bar down, he slipped a piece of cardboard between it and the base. "That's one," he muttered to himself.

Carefully, he opened the driver's door and reached across to roll down the window on the passenger side, being careful not to jar the truck. Then he went around and repeated the process on the second trap.

"That's two," he announced out loud, as he opened the passenger door very slowly. "I'm going to have a look in the bag."

"What if it's booby-trapped, too?" he heard Joe ask, behind him.

"Doesn't look like it," Frank said, easing the mouth of the bag open. Inside, he saw four large flashlight batteries and seven sticks of dynamite taped into two neat bundles, a network of wires running from the batteries to the dynamite. Gently, he lifted the bundles out of the bag, studied the wires for a minute, and then began pulling them loose. At last, he pulled a small metal cylinder out of the dynamite.

"That's it," he said, holding up the two bundles for Joe to see. "We're clean."

"Maybe," Joe said. "But let's make sure, huh?"

After searching the truck for any more surprises, they climbed in. "All set?" Joe asked. "If we're going to locate that ultralight cable, we'd better get going."

"All set, except for one thing."

Joe raised his eyebrows. "Which is?"

"I wonder," Frank replied reflectively, "whether Barbara Harris had any intention of keeping that date."

The boys spent several unsuccessful hours trying to find a piece of stainless steel cable to repair the controls on the ultralight. Finally, they stopped at a pay phone and Frank called the ultralight's manufacturer.

"Sky Streak Aviation," a woman's voice said on the other end of the line.

"My name is Frank Hardy. I was flying a Sky Streak One-oh-seven the other day, and the rudder cable broke. I need—"

But he didn't get to finish. "That's impossible, sir," the woman said confidently. "Our control cables *never* break!"

Frank chuckled. "Maybe not. But this one did, I assure you. I need a replacement."

On the other end of the line, he could hear the murmur of voices. Then the woman came back. "We hope that the break didn't cause you any inconvenience," she said. "The cable is covered by our warranty, of course. We can ship you a replacement by overnight express." She paused. "Would you mind returning the original? Our engineers would like to examine it."

Frank couldn't help smiling. "It's a deal. I'll pick up the cable at the express package depot in Armstrong, New Mexico, and return the one that broke."

It was late afternoon by the time the boys got into the truck and headed back to the Circle C. They stopped at the store in Caprock for a soda.

"Glad to see you boys," the frail little man greeted them. "Got a message for you."

"A message?" they said together, eyeing each other. What now?

"Old Charlie was in here a little while ago, looking for you."

"What did he want?" Frank asked.

"He seemed to think it was real important that you come to see him, at his place."

Joe's eyes narrowed. "How do we get there?"

"Best I can remember, after you come down

off the caprock you hit an old survey road." The storekeeper squinted, trying to think. "Take a left and go south about half a mile, and you'll come up on some ruins. That's where he's got his shack."

Just after the highway reached the bottom of the caprock, Joe spotted a rutted road, not much more than a pair of dusty tracks, leading off to the left through the mesquite. It looked as if it hadn't seen a vehicle all summer.

"That must be it," Frank said.

Joe turned down the road. Within half a mile, the caprock to their left and above them changed dramatically from a gentle slope to a high, rugged cliff. The narrow road, wide enough for only one vehicle, hugged its base.

"Some road," Joe grunted, swerving to avoid a big rock that looked as if it had tumbled off the cliff face.

Frank laughed. "I don't imagine Charlie has a whole lot of visitors," he remarked. He frowned, peering ahead. "Wonder where that dust cloud's coming from?"

Joe glanced up from the road. Up ahead, not too far, he saw a rolling dust cloud. Another storm?

No—this cloud was on the road, coming straight at them. Joe made out the front of a huge truck in the swirling dust.

Then chrome grillwork filled the whole windshield as the truck barreled straight for them.

Chapter 8

JOE SWERVED SHARPLY to the right, praying they could scrape past the huge truck. Shrub branches screeched against the sides as the pickup careened on two wheels off the road. Joe fought the wheel, gritting his teeth as they bounced around.

The pickup settled back onto four wheels, unhurt by the passing truck. When Joe looked in the mirror, all he saw was a cloud of dust.

"What was *that?*" he gasped.

"It sure wasn't the tooth fairy," Frank said, looking behind them. "Looked like a Mack truck cab without a trailer. The driver was pushing that rig at a pretty good clip."

"I wonder if that's the kind of truck they use to pull the tank trailers?" Joe asked.

"Maybe." Frank glanced over at him,

frowning. "I don't like this. It's almost as if it were waiting for us to come along."

"Let's try to follow it." Joe restarted the engine and shifted into reverse. The wheels spun, showering sand, but the pickup didn't move.

Frank climbed out and looked under the truck. "Forget about following them—we've bottomed out."

After a half hour of digging in the loose sand, the boys could finally see under the truck again. "Okay," Frank said. "Let's give it a try. I'll push."

With Frank putting his shoulder against the front grill, Joe eased out the clutch and felt the truck lurch backward onto the dirt road.

"Next stop, Charlie's place," Frank announced, hopping in. He grinned at Joe. "Let's stay on the road, huh? I'm not crazy about doing any more digging."

Joe laughed. "Tell that to the big Mack."

A half mile later, by a streambed, the boys spotted a low adobe hut with whitewashed walls and a roof made from scrap sheet metal. They parked in a dirt yard that had been swept clean. But the only signs of life were a couple of chickens and a scrawny-looking goat tethered to a post beside a battered, rusty bucket of water. The door to the hut open invitingly.

"Charlie?" Frank called through his cupped hands. "Hey, Charlie!"

Joe put two fingers to his mouth and whistled, but the only answer came from the goat, who bleated at them with a woeful sound. The boys went to the door and looked into a small, spotless room. The floor was packed dirt. Along the far wall was a blanket-covered cot. In one corner was a set of narrow shelves.

"Everything in its place," Frank said.

Joe found himself lowering his voice. "He may not have a lot, but it feels so—peaceful—in here. Almost like a church."

Frank nodded. "You're closer than you think. Those shelves over there must be Charlie's shrine," he said quietly. "Should we go in?"

"Well, he invited us," Joe said. "And the door's open. Maybe he wanted us to *see* something."

The boys stepped inside. The shelves were full of candles and handmade pottery bowls. The bowls held dried herbs, or colored sand and powders. A bundle wrapped in white goatskin took up the lowest shelf. Beside it lay a heap of rattlesnake fangs and a half-dozen snake rattles. A snakeskin hung beside the shelf.

"Looks like old Charlie had a real thing for rattlesnakes," Joe said.

"It may be a totem, or some kind of spirit guide," Frank said. "A lot of Native American beliefs deal with animals and how they can lend people their strength. Animal spirits can also teach people and protect them."

Joe's curious gaze went from the rattler fangs to the goatskin bundle. "And this?"

Frank shook his head. "That's Charlie's medicine bundle. I don't think we ought to mess with it. Whatever's in there is sacred to him."

Joe pulled his hand back. "Thanks for telling me." He was about to turn away when he saw something else. "Hey, what do you make of *this?*" he asked excitedly.

Behind the medicine bundle was an old pine board, painted with three sets of symbols. On the right was a circle with a *C* in the middle. Slightly above it were three squiggly lines, one on top of the other. On the left were three interlocking circles.

Joe frowned and pointed to the three circles. "This looks a lot like the Olympic symbol."

Frank leaned over, studying it. "If I remember my rules for naming brands, I'd say that's the Triple O."

"And that's a Circle C!" Joe exclaimed. "And that stack of squiggles—"

"They look like sound waves to me," Frank said.

"I don't think that's what Charlie means," Joe said. "Maybe he's trying to show the conflict between the two ranches."

Frank raised his eyebrows. "It's possible,"

he said. "I'd give a lot to know what Charlie really knows." He turned and started out the door. "Well, I guess there's no point in hanging out here any longer."

Outside, the goat gave them another forlorn bleat as they climbed in the truck and drove off.

At the bunkhouse on the caprock, Joe took a pizza out of the freezer and put it into the microwave, while Frank called Roy and went over the day's events. "We're going to spend the night at the bunkhouse," he said. "We've got a lot to do tomorrow."

"We do?" Joe asked as Frank hung up the phone. "And I noticed you didn't ask Roy about those symbols."

Frank shrugged as he sat down at the table for pizza. "So far, Roy hasn't been willing to say much about his relations with Oscar Owens and the Triple O. We know there are bad feelings between them." He took a bite and chewed. "I think we can find out why and how much by checking the records in the courthouse."

At nine the next morning Frank and Joe were parked on the square in the center of Armstrong. Under the stately cottonwood trees were several granite memorials and war souvenirs, including an olive-drab artillery piece and a ship's anchor. The boys climbed the steps of the impressive dome-topped courthouse. Inside, there was a three-story rotunda with a mosaic floor. On the far side of the rotunda was a glass door with County Clerk on it in gold letters.

Behind the marble counter of the county clerk's office, a grandmotherly woman greeted them. "May I help you?" Then she gave Joe a startled look. "You look *just* like my grandson," she said. "Isn't that a coincidence?"

Joe ducked his head and gave her a shy, embarrassed grin. "Yes, ma'am," he said, sounding interested. "Does he live around here?"

In a minute the woman had treated them to a description of her whole family. She had obviously taken a liking to Joe. Then, suddenly, she remembered that they might be there on business. "Now, what can I help you find this morning?"

Frank leaned forward. "We'd like to examine the deeds to a couple of ranches up near Caprock—the Circle C and the Triple O. We'd also like to see copies of their grazing leases."

"Mineral leases as well?" the woman asked helpfully.

"What? Oh, yes, please," Frank replied.

In a few minutes she returned with a pile of folders. The deed to the Triple O was a simple document, certifying that the land had been deeded to the Owens family eighty years ago by the government. The other files concerned the Circle C. Roy had begun purchasing the land about twenty years ago. There were some grazing and mineral leases dating back before that time, but many were much more recent.

"It looks kind of complicated," Joe remarked, while Frank began to copy the dates of the leases.

"But that's the way people around here acquire land." The woman smiled at Joe. "In fact, Mr. Carlson has been very successful with his ranching operations."

"What about these mineral rights?" Frank asked. "Are they worth anything?"

The woman shrugged. "Not much, probably. Nobody's located anything in that area. Mr. Carlson probably picked them up to prevent exploration, which can be pretty destructive. The oil companies have to pay damages, but some ranchers don't think it's enough."

Joe smiled at her willingness to answer questions. "I'll bet you get all the land gossip," he said. "Have you heard anything about the Circle C and the Triple O—you know, problems, anything like that?"

The woman hesitated. "Well, of course, it's not a matter of public record, and I probably shouldn't say anything. But I heard that Mr. Carlson and Mr. Owens banged heads a few years back, when they shared some leased pasture where the two ranches join." She smiled. "My husband worked at the auction barn that spring, and he said that everybody was talking about how many Circle C mama cows had calves with Triple O brands."

"You mean, Owens put his brand on Circle C calves?" Joe asked, sounding shocked.

"Of course it wasn't ever proven," she added hastily. "But I know for a fact that after that, Mr. Carlson wouldn't have anything to do with Mr. Owens."

Frank closed the folders. "Is any of the land around here owned by Native Americans?"

The woman shook her head. "No, the reservations are all west and north of here."

"We heard that some of them consider part of the caprock to be their sacred territory," Joe said.

"Oh, you probably mean Lawson's Bluff." She turned to the topographic map on the wall behind her and pointed to a section that jutted out from the ridge of the caprock. "Actually, it's on the Circle C, just north of the boundary with the Triple O. It's called Lawson's Bluff because the Lawson family was killed there in an Indian raid." She shook her head. "But the Indians don't have any legal claim to it."

Frank folded his notes and put them in his pocket. "Thanks for your help," he said.

Joe leaned forward, giving her a special

smile. "Tell your grandson 'hi' for me," he said.

"I'll do that," the woman promised.

"Why don't you give Barbara a call," Frank said to Joe as they left the courthouse. "See if she can join us for a cup of coffee."

Joe frowned. "You still think she might have had something to do with that booby trap, huh?"

"You've got to admit that it was quite a coincidence." Frank watched the annoyed expression on his brother's face. Joe liked to trust pretty girls. Sometimes that got him—and Frank—into trouble. "At least she can explain some of this stuff about land leases and dirty tricks. We could use a clue or two."

With a sharp nod, Joe agreed and headed for a pay phone. Joe reported that Barbara would meet them in an hour. The two boys walked down the street to the express package depot to pick up the cable for the ultralight.

They strolled into a clothing store and each of them bought new boots and a western hat.

"We've still got some time to kill," Frank said after they left and were passing a combination pawn shop and sporting goods store. "Let's take a look in here."

"Hey," Joe said as they stepped inside, "this place could arm a banana republic." The shelves were filled with surplus military equipment.

Frank went to the counter. "Do you handle army surplus ammo?" he asked the clerk.

"Got some M-sixteen and some forty-five." The man opened a glass case. "What are you looking for?"

"Just trying to identify some empties I found," Frank said, scanning the case. The M16 ammo was a .223 caliber, much smaller than the casings he'd found at the stock tank. Then he spotted some larger, tarnished, bottleneck cartridges. The bullet tips were painted black.

"Armor-piercing three-oh-three British," the clerk said, following Frank's glance. He took one out and handed it to him. On the base was the number forty-three.

Joe looked over Frank's shoulder. "Seems to me that the shells we saw were tapered like this, but the shoulder was shorter," he said.

The clerk nodded. "Yep, it was a three-oh-three. Looks that way after it's fired. Packs quite a punch, too—armor-piercing bullets have a steel core." He smacked his fist hard into his open palm. "Designed to smash right through armor plate. It fits the Lee-Enfield rifles the British used in World War Two." He pointed to a heavy-looking, old warhorse of a rifle hanging on the wall. The unfinished wooden hand guard and stock extended almost to the end of the barrel, while the magazine was sharply tapered.

Frank handed back the cartridge. "Sell many of these?" he asked casually.

"Not a whole lot," the guy said, putting it back. "But a fella came in the other day and bought a couple of boxes." He shut the case.

"Somebody you knew?" Joe asked.

The clerk shook his head. "Never saw him before." He studied the boys. "Got a reason for asking?"

"Just curious," Frank said. He lifted his hand in a wave, and they left.

"Well, now that we know the gun we're looking for," Joe said with satisfaction, "it shouldn't be too hard to find."

Frank gave a short laugh and pointed to the dusty pickups parked in a row along the curb. Each one had a gun rack in the back window, and every rack held at least one rifle. "Knowing what we're looking for is one thing," he said. "Finding it is another."

They'd been at the restaurant only a few minutes when Barbara came in. She'd pinned her hair up and traded her jeans for a denim skirt.

"Hi, guys," she greeted them, sliding into the booth beside Joe. "What's new?"

Joe smiled at her quick laugh and easy, open western way. He wouldn't mind making friends with her, but what they needed right then was information. Barbara grinned at him, her eyes crinkling when she smiled. No way could Joe believe she had anything to do with the bomb in the truck.

Frank started leading the conversation, telling Barbara about their visit to Caprock Charlie's place.

"I'm jealous," she told him. "Charlie's always friendly to me but never talks much. Too bad. He'd be a term paper in anthropology. I've heard that he's the last of his tribe, and it would be a shame to lose the knowledge he has."

"Do you think he's angry at the people around here?" Frank asked. "Maybe he thinks Roy Carlson shouldn't be ranching around the holy place on Lawson's Bluff."

"You don't mean you think *he's* behind all the trouble on the Circle C?" Barbara showed that she knew about the Carlsons' problems. But she mentioned no more than she might have heard on the county grapevine. Joe breathed a sigh of relief.

Then Frank changed the subject abruptly. "We were over at the courthouse this morning, looking at the mineral leases," he said. "Do you suppose that minerals—gold, oil, uranium—might have something to do with this?"

Barbara's mouth tightened. "Maybe," she said guardedly. "And maybe not." She pushed her coffee cup away. "Time to get back to work." She glanced at Joe. "You're picking me up for the dance tonight, right?"

"At eight," Joe said, but he didn't give her his usual grin. He didn't *feel* like grinning. Obviously, Barbara knew something. But what?

When Barbara left, the boys headed out for the pickup. This time, they inspected it carefully before they opened the doors and climbed in.

"Well," Frank said, eyeing Joe, "what do you think?"

"I don't know," Joe said glumly. He'd still bet on his hunch that Barbara was okay, but maybe he wouldn't be willing to go with long odds. *What* did she know?

The boys made a quick trip back to the ranch. Frank removed the damaged cable from the ultralight, while Joe went over the rest of the aircraft.

Frank had pulled the cable out and was studying the broken end when Joe interrupted him. "Looks like you've lost a rivet here," he said.

Frank turned. Joe was pointing to a perfectly round hole in the bottom of the tail strut tube, through which the control lines passed.

"That's funny," Frank said. "There shouldn't be any rivets there."

He explored the hole with his fingers and

then reached around the tube. There was a matching hole on the other side. It was rough-edged and something was stuck in it. He worked it loose, then took it to the barn door, where he could examine it in the light. What he was holding was a small flake of copper.

With a frown, he took another look at the tip of the cable he'd just removed. Then he turned to Joe, his face bleak.

"This cable didn't break on its own," he said. "It was cut—by an armor-piercing bullet!"

Chapter 9

"A BULLET?" Joe exclaimed, staring at the frayed steel strands with a smear of metal on the ends. "A bullet made of copper?"

"That comes from the jacket of that armor-piercing bullet. The steel core, of course, passed through and kept on going."

"Talk about a lucky shot." Joe's face grew grim. "This means that the guy who did this was on to us from the minute we got here."

"That's what it looks like," Frank agreed. "Maybe the shot was meant as a warning—but if that's the case, they were wasting ammo. I couldn't have heard a shot over the racket that engine makes."

Joe turned back to the ultralight. "I haven't spotted any other damage."

Frank was looking at the hole. "And I don't

think the shot did any structural damage to the strut. If you'll give me a hand, I'll route the new cable and take this thing for a test flight." His eyes narrowed. "And after that, I think we ought to give Oscar Owens a visit."

The new cable worked perfectly, and the test flight was beautiful. The boys stopped at the ranch house to ask directions to the Triple O.

Roy wasn't very enthusiastic about their plan to talk to Owens, but he finally agreed. "If you go a couple of miles past the old homestead," he told them, "you'll come to a fence and a cattle guard. That's the boundary with the Triple O."

"So you can drive from one ranch to the other without going onto the highway," Joe mused.

Roy shrugged. "The road's maintained by the county," he said. "Anybody's free to use it."

"Then the tank truck could have been driven here through the Triple O," Frank said. "Or from there?"

"I suppose," Roy replied. "But it could just as easily have come in from the highway, or down one of the old survey roads."

The boys got into the yellow pickup and headed south. "Well, what do you make of all this?" Joe asked, steering to avoid a huge pothole in the road.

"We have too many loose ends to suit me."

Frank sounded frustrated. "But the worst of it is that we're still short of a motive. If it's revenge, the main suspect—Jake Grimes—is laid up with a broken leg. If it's greed, Oscar Owens is a good candidate. But what could he be after? Marginal grazing land and worthless mineral leases hardly justify kidnapping and three counts of attempted murder."

He shook his head. "If it's a desire to get back a hunk of sacred territory, our suspect is an old man whose only weapon is a gourd rattle. To round things off, we've got a couple of suspects who don't seem to have any motive at all—an attractive young lady and a reliable ranch hand who might have engineered his own disappearance."

"Speaking of suspects," Joe said, "look over there." He pointed to a sand dune several hundred yards away. At the top of the dune stood a lone figure, wearing a straw sombrero. Between them and the figure was a sea of waist-high sagebrush. Joe pulled over and the Hardys got out and stood beside the truck. The figure on the dune didn't move.

"Looks like Charlie's keeping tabs on us again," Joe remarked. "It's really weird how he always seems to be in the right place at the right time—like he knows what's going to happen."

"The people who study ESP have a name

for that," Frank told him. "They call it precognition."

"Suppose we ought to hike over there and have a visit?"

"I don't think there's much point in it. If Charlie wanted to talk to us, he'd make an effort to come down here by the road. Anyway, we'd never get the truck through that sagebrush, and he'd be long gone by the time we could get to him on foot." He grinned. "My guess is that he'll show up again—when *he* feels like it."

As if to confirm Frank's guess, the figure vanished just then behind the dune.

The boys got back in the truck. After another twenty minutes on the rough road, they came to a cattle guard, a metal grid buried in the ground that they had to drive over. Joe slowed. A white sign fastened to a post announced that they were entering the Triple O ranch, and that trespassers would be prosecuted.

"We're not trespassing, we're visiting," Joe muttered, shoving the accelerator down. The truck leaped forward.

Three or four miles beyond the Hardys could see a ranch complex up on a ridge. The main house was large and single storied, Spanish style. Its whitewashed walls gleamed in the afternoon sun, under the neat geometry of an orange clay tile roof. As they got closer, they could see a large man standing on the veranda, looking in their direction.

"I guess they're expecting us," Joe said.

By the time they pulled up the big man was standing in the front yard. Frank recognized him—Nat Wilkin, the foreman who'd helped search for Jerry.

"What's up, guys?" he asked. "Anything new on Jerry?"

"Afraid not, Nat," Frank said. "We'd like to see Mr. Owens."

At that moment the door behind Nat opened and an older man stepped out. He wore jeans and a work shirt, with a bandanna tied neatly around his throat. "Well, now you're seeing him," he said. "Nobody can call me unneighborly."

Oscar Owens smiled at the Hardys. "So you're the guys asking all those questions all over Armstrong County." He opened the door and led the boys down a wide hall and into a spacious room furnished with several leather armchairs and a large oak desk. "Now, what can I do for you two?" he asked, settling into the chair behind his desk.

"You know that Jerry Greene is still missing, of course," Frank began cautiously.

"Sure, I know," Owens said, with what sounded like genuine sympathy. "Too bad. My guess is that he got thrown, wandered around, and then the next day lost his bearings in that dust storm." He shook his head. "It was a bad one—one of the worst in a couple of years."

"But why would he still be wandering the next day in the storm?" Joe wanted to know. "Also, Ray says Jerry was a good rider."

Owens nodded. "Even a good rider can get thrown if his horse gets spooked. He was like his father—a good man. It doesn't seem likely that he'd wander off, the way some do."

"The Circle C has been pretty well searched," Frank said. "We wondered if you'd mind if we had a look on the Triple O."

Owens lost some of his good humor. "I don't see any harm in it. But you'd better let me know so I can have one of my hands go with you. It's awful easy to get lost around here if you don't know the country." He gave them a measured look. "No point in us having to go on another search—for you two."

Frank wondered briefly whether that was a threat, but the man's eyes still seemed friendly. "Maybe we could start in the morning."

Owens nodded. "No need to hurry," he said regretfully. "If Greene's out there, there's not much chance that he's alive." He pushed the chair away from his desk and started to stand up.

"Have you had any truck traffic down here lately?" Joe asked, carefully casual.

Owens sat back down, giving Joe a long, hard look. "As a matter of fact, my hands say they've seen some tracks. Maybe a stock truck took a wrong turn. Why do you ask?"

Frank shrugged, his eyes on Owens's face. "It was a big truck that dumped salt water into that tank," he said quietly.

Owens just nodded. "You know, I've had some trouble with Roy Carlson," he said. "That nonsense with the fences is just the latest. But things have been going worse for Roy. His horses pulled up lame, and after that came the dead cows."

He shook his head. "I can't see Roy hauling in a tanker load of salt water to kill his own stock." A slow, angry red flush moved up his face. "And I know *I* had nothing to do with it."

The silence was thick. "Well, I guess we got what we came for," Frank finally said. He stood up.

Owens didn't even show them to the door.

On the way out Frank spotted a gun rack on the wall by the door, filled with a variety of shotguns and deer rifles. Something about one rifle caught Frank's attention. The gun had a polished wooden stock that extended halfway down the shiny black barrel—and an odd magazine. It was wedge shaped, tapered sharply from the back to the front.

Frank stepped over and picked up the rifle. As he hefted it, he saw a stamp, just in front of the bolt action. It was the broad arrow, the British governmental sign.

"What are you doing with that?" a sharp voice came from behind them.

Owens came up to the door and snatched the gun from Frank. "I brought this home from the war," he said angrily. "It's my favorite gun—and I'm not going to have some kid steal it." He raised his voice. "Nat!"

The foreman appeared in the doorway as Owens pointed at the Hardys. "See these two off the ranch."

Joe glanced at Frank curiously as they were escorted to their truck. "What's the story about that gun?"

"I guess you didn't get a chance to see it clearly," Frank answered in a low voice. "It's a British Three-oh-three, Mark Three Lee-Enfield." He glanced over his shoulder to where Owens was standing on the porch, holding the rifle.

"That's the gun that shot me out of the air."

Chapter 10

"GUYS, I DON'T KNOW what happened in there," Nat Wilkin said as the Hardys got into their pickup. "But I do want to apologize for Mr. Owens. He just hasn't been himself lately."

"It's his ranch," Joe said, starting the engine. "And we're getting off it."

As the Triple O ranch house disappeared behind them, Joe shook his head. "The way Owens blew up over that rifle—he'd have to be a complete nut case to call attention to it if he'd used it on you." He swerved to miss a steer that had wandered onto the road and stood watching them with what looked like antagonism. "On the other hand," he added, "how many of those souvenir guns would there be in this area?"

Frank looked out the window. Nat Wilkin was following them in another truck. "Yet the man's reaction to the dirty tricks sounded genuine. I can't see him taking target practice on the ultralight." He sighed. "It just doesn't jibe—all we really know about Owens is that he has a violent temper."

Joe was momentarily distracted by a roadrunner, big as a rooster, that jumped out of the ditch. It zoomed down the road ahead of them, going as fast as the pickup. "What would Owens's motive be? Drive Roy out of business? Get control of the federal land?"

"A grazing lease for near-desert? That doesn't wash," Frank said thoughtfully.

"What about the mineral leases? Suppose Owens knows something nobody else knows?"

"It doesn't seem likely," Frank said doubtfully. "The big oil companies must have surveyed this area years back." He frowned. "Although—maybe Barbara knows something about those mineral leases. She cut the conversation off when I brought them up."

Joe glanced at his watch, then pushed the accelerator down. "Speaking of Barbara, we'd better head back and change—if we want to get to the dance tonight, that is."

Barbara's house was a small, yellow-painted frame house in a well-kept, older part of Armstrong. As the Hardys drove up the quiet street, they saw a red four-wheel-drive pickup parked in front.

"Well, looks like she's home," Joe said, turning off the ignition. He gave his brother a slow smile. "So, do we kick in the door and interrogate her?"

Frank grinned back. "What are you asking me for? I'm just riding shotgun. *You're* the one with the date." He settled back in the seat and settled his new cowboy hat over his eyes. "I'll wait here. But if you're not out in ten minutes, I'm calling the sheriff."

Joe laughed. "Ten minutes, huh? I guess I can handle that." He got out of the truck, giving his boots a quick rub, and started up the walk.

"I'm coming," a voice called in response to Joe's knock. The door opened and Barbara stood there, giving him a look. "Just like a real cowboy," she said, grinning at Joe's clothes.

He looked down at his fancy plaid shirt, fresh jeans, and new cowboy boots, then at Barb's plain T-shirt and comfortable jeans. "A little overdressed, huh?" he asked.

"Oh, you'll be fine. Every girl in town will want to dance with you."

Barbara's excited face showed she had something more important on her mind than a dance. "There's something I want to show you—" She looked around. "Where's Frank? I want *him* to see this, too."

"He's out in the truck, waiting for us," Joe said, puzzled. "See what?" He glanced past her. On one side was the living room, which seemed empty. At the end of a short hallway was the kitchen, empty, too, as far as he could tell.

"But he'll want to see this," Barbara insisted, sounding impatient. "Really, Joe, I think this is something you *both*—"

"Why don't you show me first," Joe suggested, beginning to feel faintly uneasy. He *knew* this couldn't be a trap, but if it was, it was better to have Frank out in the truck.

Barbara stood back and opened the door wider. "Okay," she said, sounding resigned. "Come on. I'll show you." She reached for his hand and pulled him quickly into the house.

Nervously, Joe threw a quick glance behind the door as she shut it. Nothing. And definitely nothing in the living room, either.

Barbara pulled him down the hall and into the kitchen, where the table was piled with yellowing chart paper, like the kind he'd seen used in a polygraph machine. The paper was covered with rows and rows of weird-looking squiggly lines.

Suddenly Joe had a flash of the strange symbols he'd seen at Charlie's shack. Stacks of wiggly lines—these were very similar to the ones Charlie had painted.

"What's all this stuff?" he asked.

"This is what I want to show you," Barbara said, sounding excited again. "I've been working all afternoon on them, ever since I left you and Frank at the restaurant."

She spread out the papers. "After Frank asked about the mineral leases, something clicked. So I went down to the basement at the Bureau of Land Management office and dug out these old logs. Most of them date back to the 1930s. From the looks of them, I'd guess that nobody's examined them in years." She gave him a modest smile. "You can call me brilliant, if you want to."

"Brilliant?" Joe laughed. "Maybe I'd better call you cross-eyed. What's this mess of old paper? And what are all these squiggles?"

"This 'mess of old paper,' " Barbara told him with a little annoyance, "is a batch of ancient *seismograph* logs." She ran a finger along the wavy lines. "And those squiggles are records of soundings that indicate where certain mineral deposits are located."

Joe shook his head. "I still don't get it."

Barbara's dark eyes were dancing with excitement. "Unless I'm dead wrong, Joe, the Circle C is floating on an ocean of oil!"

Chapter 11

"THIS IS INCREDIBLE!" Joe wrapped an arm around Barbara's shoulder and gave her a huge hug.

Suddenly he remembered that Frank was waiting in the truck.

"Hang on a sec," he said, and hurried to the front door. He stepped outside and closed the door behind him to show Frank that nobody had the drop on him. Then he beckoned his brother to come in and stepped back inside, leaving the door open. In a moment Frank had joined them in the kitchen.

"Look what Barbara found in the basement of the BLM." Joe pointed to the piles of paper on the kitchen table. He shot him a triumphant what-did-I-tell-you look. "She thought of them when you mentioned the mineral leases this morning."

"What are they? Old seismograph logs?" Frank asked, picking up one of the long sheets and studying it. His face was expressionless, but Joe could tell that it was excitement that was tensing the muscles in his brother's jaw. "Somebody's already explored for oil in the area, then?"

"Yes." Barbara nodded. "These logs were made in the Caprock area, back around 1930. I'm not exactly sure of the coordinates, but as far as I can tell, the exploration took place on the south end of the old Circle C, near the sand hills."

"Can you read these?" Frank asked, still studying them.

"I took a geology course last year, and we did a lot of work with seismograph reports." Barbara pointed to the set of squiggles that Frank was looking at. "Those wavy lines, for instance—they indicate a big salt dome."

"What's salt got to do with oil?" Joe asked.

"A lot," Barbara told him. "Under great heat and pressure, salt deposits ooze around, sort of like molasses. When the salt finds a weak spot underground, it rises up like a giant bubble until it's stopped by harder rock. As the salt bubble heads upward, oil can flow up too, collecting around the top of the dome. So when you find a formation like this, you'll often find a pool of oil at the top."

Frank grinned. "As I recall, Spindletop was a salt dome."

Joe frowned. "Spindletop?"

Barbara nodded. "The first—and the biggest—oil field discovered in the Southwest, back in 1901. It was a salt dome formation."

Joe thumped the pile of yellowing logs. "But if they found *this* dome back in 1930," he asked, "why didn't they sink any wells?"

"Look at these notes," Barbara said, pointing to a faded pencil scribble in the margin of the log Frank was looking at. "The top of the dome is about eleven thousand feet below ground level."

Frank whistled. "There's your answer, Joe. Back in the thirties, nobody could drill that deep. The technology was still pretty primitive."

"Right," Barbara chimed in. "And even if they could've sunk a well that deep, the price of oil was so low that it wouldn't have justified the cost."

"But the price of oil is a lot higher now." Joe leaned back thoughtfully against the refrigerator.

"And they're drilling that deep, and deeper, if the formation looks good enough," Barbara said. "Especially in the U.S., with this push to find domestic oil."

"These seismographs"—Frank tapped the log on the table—"they're made by exploding subsurface charges and measuring the shock waves. Right?"

"You mean, bombs?" said Joe.

"These logs were probably made that way," Barbara told them. "Nowadays, geologists generally use large, specially equipped trucks. They drop heavy weights that cause the vibrations."

With growing excitement, Joe looked at Frank. He could see what his brother was getting at.

"But they could still use the old method, couldn't they?" Joe asked. "And the people who were setting the charges would have to know how to use dynamite, wouldn't they?"

Barbara nodded. "If you didn't have the new equipment, I guess you'd *have* to do it the old way." She looked puzzled. "Why?"

Joe grinned triumphantly. Barbara couldn't be faking this kind of innocence. Whatever dirty dealing was going on, she wasn't involved in it.

"Oh, we've just been getting a lot of dynamite lately," he said casually. "Somebody stuck some in the stove at the old homestead on the Circle C, where we were camping. Then they wired it to blow up our pickup when the door opened."

Barbara's dark eyes widened in horror.

"You mean, somebody's been trying to *kill* the two of you?"

Joe laughed. "Either that, or they just like the noise dynamite makes when it blows up."

"Speaking of the noise dynamite makes," Frank broke in, "do you remember the thunder we heard that first night at the homestead shack? I'll bet we were hearing somebody setting off an explosive charge."

Barbara let out her breath. "Somebody must be looking for oil!"

"Sounds that way," Joe said. He frowned. "What would a seismography site look like? A bunch of big holes blasted in the ground?"

Barbara shook her head. "Not at all. The bore holes are only about three inches in diameter, maybe a hundred feet deep or so, and about a hundred feet apart. But on the surface, all you'd see is the hole, with a small pile of drill tailings—dirt the drill rig brought up."

"What about the drill rig?" Frank wanted to know. "Would they need to bring in a big one?"

"Not to drill small test holes—they can drill them dry, with a rig that can be hauled on a truck."

Joe scratched his head. He could see that they were getting somewhere. But there was a big hole in their logic. "But what good would it do somebody to find out about the oil?" he asked. "It would still cost them a fortune to get it out, wouldn't it?"

"But you could get plenty rich without drilling," Barbara pointed out. "Once you've got reliable evidence that the oil is there, you buy the mineral rights or leases for next to nothing. Then you take your evidence to any big oil company and watch the value of your leases shoot sky-high."

"That explains the secrecy, but it still doesn't explain all the nasty tricks," Joe said. "Roy owns the middle part of the Circle C—that's where you're saying most of the oil is. He leases the northern end from the state—"

"And the southern end from the federal government," Frank finished for him. "All the trouble has been on the federal land—to keep him from renewing his grazing lease."

"But why?" Barbara said. "Oil drilling isn't like strip mining. There'd be lots of room for the cattle to graze around the oil wells."

"Unless"—Joe snapped his fingers—"they don't *want* Roy to know about the oil wells!" He swiveled around to face Frank and Barbara. "Try this out. Part of the oil deposit extends onto the federal land. If nobody's grazing out there, who'd know that somebody was drilling for oil?"

"And maybe sucking it up from someone else's land!" Frank nodded. "That would finally nail down a motive. I think we'd better check this out. *Pronto*".

"Right," Joe said.

"Hold on, cowboys!" Barbara said, grabbing them both by the arm. "If you're running around out there in the desert tonight, who's taking me to the dance?"

The brothers exchanged reluctant looks.

"You won't find anything out there in the dark, except for a few coyotes," Barbara said, bullying them good-naturedly. "And, anyway, you're going to need *my* help."

"Your help?" Frank asked. "Hey, wait a minute. I don't think—"

Barbara planted her feet firmly. "You don't know your way around that desert. *I* do. You'd get lost in a minute. *I* won't." She gave them a pitying look. "You've never even seen a seismography site. *I* have. *I* know what we're looking for, and you don't."

"The girl's got a point," Joe admitted to Frank, trying to keep from laughing.

"Sounds like blackmail to me," Frank muttered.

Barbara gave them both an angelic smile. "It's called compromise," she said sweetly. "Tomorrow we search. Tonight we party! You guys haven't lived until you've danced the cotton-eyed Joe."

Frank grinned in mock surrender. "Okay,"

he said. "Tonight we party. First thing in the morning we look for bad guys."

It was just before dawn when Joe heard the sound of a jeep outside the bunkhouse. The horn honked twice.

Frank lifted the curtain. "She's here," he announced. "Right on time, too."

"She *would* be," Joe grunted, trying to overcome his sleepiness with a second cup of coffee. He wiggled his toes. His feet were *still* sore from dancing the cotton-eyed Joe.

While Frank called the Circle C ranch house to tell Roy where they were going, Joe stepped outside into the chill, predawn dark. He rubbed his eyes, wondering if he was still dreaming. Barbara's jeep was painted a bright candy-apple red, with fancy black stripes and a black roll bar. Barb herself looked as if she were dressed for work, in a khaki jumpsuit and hiking boots, with a soft hat mashed down over her hair. A pair of binoculars were slung around her neck.

She already had a map spread out as the Hardys climbed into the jeep. "We'll be heading across the caprock, then down into the sand hills." Barbara traced the route with a finger.

"I took another look at the logs this morning before I left," she said. "And I think this is where they tested back in the thirties. It seems like a good spot to start our search—then we can work our way east. The road peters out at this point—" She jabbed at the map.

"The old homestead isn't far to the west, but it's all loose sand. No way to get across in a vehicle, so it's not likely they were doing seismographic blasting in that direction. It would be murder to cross it during the day, on foot."

She grinned, proud of her detecting. "So, buckle up and hang on. The road gets a little rough from here on out."

She gunned the engine and headed off fast down a dirt track that Joe hadn't noticed behind the bunkhouse. Boy, she wasn't kidding about it being rough, Joe thought, waking up in a hurry as he grabbed for something to hold on to. At the edge of the caprock, the trail turned south and then dropped over the edge, angling steeply, doubling back a couple of times as it zigzagged down. It was rocky and badly rutted.

Barbara downshifted but she didn't slow down, and Joe, bouncing in the front seat, gritted his teeth and held his breath as they plummeted toward the bottom. At the foot of the cliff, the track wound through the sagebrush and then intersected with a hard-packed gravel road. Barbara pushed the accelerator to the floor.

"That detour saved us about twelve miles," she shouted over the roar of the jeep. She patted the dash affectionately. "Tinkerbell *loves* to fly down cliffs. It's her favorite thing."

"Tinkerbell?" Frank blinked.

Barbara laughed. "Isn't that a great name? It's definitely *her.*"

Great, Joe thought wryly. Tinkerbell had saved thirty minutes—and only scared about five years of life out of him. But his admiration for Barbara reached even higher. She was some driver.

For the next thirty minutes, they rocketed through a maze of roads and dirt trails, through the scrubby mesquite trees and low sand hills. At each intersection, Barbara twisted the wheel without hesitation. Joe couldn't help being glad they'd left the driving to her. All the roads looked alike to him. He wouldn't have known which way to turn.

At last the jeep slowed to a reasonable speed and they could talk comfortably.

Frank leaned forward and tapped Barbara on the shoulder. "Stop!" he commanded. Seconds later he was vaulting out of the jeep and scrambling up the sandy slope beside the road.

Joe saw what had caught his brother's attention. A little way up the slope were a series of wavy marks, like squiggles traced in the sand by some unseen finger.

"Hey, that looks like the symbol we saw in Charlie's shack!" Joe opened his door and jumped out.

"What symbol?" Barbara asked, standing up in the jeep and putting her binoculars to her eyes. "What's Frank looking at?"

Right then, Joe became aware of a strange buzzing noise somewhere down at his feet. It sounded like a clock radio alarm buzzing, and he glanced down, puzzled.

The next thing he knew, someone was hitting him in a flying tackle.

Joe tried to turn in midair, tried to grab for his attacker. Instead, he found himself going facedown into the gritty sand.

Chapter 12

JOE LANDED HARD, but in a second he was on his feet, glaring at Barbara and spitting sand. "What's the big idea?" he demanded. "Where I come from, they call that clipping!"

Barbara chuckled as she looked down at him. "Around here, they call it saving your hide, cowboy. That sidewinder almost got you."

Barbara pointed under a sagebrush, where a pale, leathery tail with a rattle on it was just wriggling out of sight. "Only a greenhorn goes messing with sidewinder tracks without looking for the sidewinder."

Frank joined them. "So that was a rattlesnake track I was looking at, huh?"

"Give that man an A in herpetology." Barb bent over and traced out a wavy track in the sand. "Somewhere back in its evolution, the sidewinder rattlesnake learned how to get around in loose sand. It throws its body in loops out to one side, turns its head that way, and literally moves sideways. That's how it got its name."

Joe brushed sand off his jeans. "Those tracks look like the symbol on Charlie's wall. And we guessed he's really into snakes." He quickly told Barbara what they had found in Charlie's hut—the snakeskin, the rattles and fangs, and the crude sketch on the old pine board.

"I wouldn't be surprised if it was his symbol for a sidewinder," Barbara said, nodding.

They got back in the jeep and Barbara spun it around. As they drove, the boys kept watch for any sign of recent traffic.

Frank pointed to a trail of tire tracks that led off through the mesquite. "These had to be made after the storm. Let's check them out."

Expertly Barbara shoved the jeep into low gear and headed in the direction Frank was pointing. The tracks wound into the sagebrush for about fifty yards. Then they ended in a clearing.

"Hey, look," Joe shouted, jumping out. On the ground were several pairs of thin yellow wire strands—like the wire they'd found in the truck bomb. These were partly buried in the sand, but Joe could see they led off in several directions.

Barbara pulled up on one end of a wire. "This must have been the firing position," she said. "Let's see what's on the other end of this."

The three of them followed the wire through the thorny vegetation. With its feathery leaves, mesquite might be pretty to look at, Joe decided, and it might even be good to eat, if you were a goat. But it definitely wasn't fun to get scraped by the long, sharp thorns. He winced and muttered as one of them made a deep scratch on his arm.

Barbara was pulling up the wire where it was partly buried under drifted sand. Following it, they came across a small pile of fresh red clay powder. The wire disappeared down a three-inch hole beside the pile.

"That, gentlemen," Barbara said in an authoritative voice, "is a bore hole. If we traced out the other wires, we'd find one of these at the end of each of them."

"Well, I guess we've found the evidence to back up our motive," Joe said. "What now?"

Before the others could answer, a horse's whinny pierced the air—from very close by.

"We've got company!" Frank whispered.

Quickly the three of them slipped behind the cover of some dense mesquite bushes and crouched close to the ground. A minute or two passed. There was only the sound of the wind. The air, which had been chilly when they set out, was beginning to warm up as the morning sun climbed higher in the sky.

"Maybe we shouldn't have left the jeep alone," Joe said. "This far from civilization, we'd be in trouble if somebody took it out."

"Right," Barbara whispered. "It'd be a long walk to *anywhere* from here."

Frank nodded, agreeing. "Let's swing out wide and double back to the jeep."

The going was rough. They hunkered down, trying to keep to the cover of the low mesquite. It was hard to keep their footing on the drifted sand. By the time they crept back to the clearing where the jeep was parked, Joe was covered with sweat. His eyes ached from straining for any sign of movement that might give away the presence of their uninvited guest.

"No sign of horses or riders," Barbara whispered as they lay on their stomachs on a sandy rise, surveying the clearing.

"Looks okay to me, too," Joe said, wiping the sweat out of his eyes with his sleeve. He started to get to his feet. "I'm tired of this creepy crawly stuff. Let's—"

Ka-bam! A shotgun blast raked the clearing, kicking up geysers of dust. Joe dropped to the ground, shielding his head with his arms. He waited for another blast, but nothing happened. A half minute later they heard the snort of a horse and muffled hoofbeats. It sounded as if whoever had fired at them was heading away at a fast clip. Joe decided to stay put for another minute, just in case.

He glanced at Barbara. "You okay?" he whispered.

"I'm fine," she answered, then turned her head. "Frank?"

There was a silence, and Joe raised his head, suddenly scared. Had Frank been hit?

"I'm fine." Frank had slithered down the small hill. "But Tinkerbell isn't. They blew away her radiator."

Joe saw a stream of green liquid spurting from several holes in the front of the jeep. A growing pool had already formed under the jeep's engine.

"Poor Tink!" Barbara exclaimed. "How can we plug all those leaks!"

Frank's voice stopped her. "Forget it. Even if we could stop the holes and there was enough coolant left in the radiator, the plugs would never hold under pressure. Tinkerbell's had it. She's not going anywhere without a new radiator."

"Looks like we'll be stuck here for a while," Barbara said calmly. "But I always carry an extra couple of gallons of water in the back of the jeep, and we still have the CB. So let's have a drink and call for help."

"Okay," Frank agreed. "But just in case

we're not alone, I say that only one of us checks it out. You two stay here."

Before Joe could protest, Frank headed for the jeep, bent over in a half crouch. Cautiously, he circled the vehicle, then, confident that their attackers had gone, he straightened up, reached into the back of the jeep, and grabbed two plastic jugs.

"Empty," he said, tossing them on the ground.

"Impossible!" Barbara exclaimed in dismay. "I filled them before I left!"

"Then somebody must have emptied them." Joe scrambled hurriedly to his feet. "And if they got the water, maybe they also got—"

"Right." Frank's voice was quiet, but Joe could hear the underlying tension in it. He held up the microphone cord for the CB. The cord was there, but the mike was gone.

Joe wiped the sweat from his eyes and glanced up at the sun. It was already burning down on them and noon was still hours away. "What do we do now? We're at least fifteen miles from help, on foot in the desert. It's going to be murder out there in a couple of hours."

"That," Frank said in a grim voice, "is exactly what our attacker had in mind."

Chapter 13

"THEY REALLY DID a number on us." Frank's face was worried as he started back up the slope. "We're stranded, with no way to call for help, and our whole water supply is sinking into the sand."

Barbara glanced up at the blazing sun. "They might as well have shot us dead."

"Oh, no," Frank said grimly. "If someone found us dead of thirst, it could be an accident—especially if they come back and wreck the jeep. That wouldn't work if we had bullet holes."

"How did these guys know where we were?" Joe asked. "Did they follow us?"

Barbara looked embarrassed. "All they needed was a lookout up on the caprock with binoculars and a radio. The dust we were kicking up would send them a smoke signal. They'd know just where we were going and radio a warning ahead."

Joe felt his anger rising—mostly at himself. "These guys have been one step ahead of us ever since we got here." And one reason they'd kept their lead had been the way he'd let himself get distracted with Barbara. If he'd thought about the case instead, they might not be in this fix.

Barbara patted him on the shoulder. "Loosen up, cowboy. You don't know this country. I guess it should have occurred to *me* that somebody might not want us poking around, looking for seismography sites. I might have been a little more careful about the dust I was raising."

Frank nodded. "We got what we came for," he reminded Joe. "Now we have a motive for what's happened at Roy's place. And even if we *never* find out who's behind it, we've got enough to sink their plan. Once Roy hears about the oil, he can protect his ranch—and what's under it."

Joe sat back on his heels. "Not only that, we have a very solid suspect. I'd like to ask Nat Wilkin if Owens has been out using his three-oh-three lately." He frowned. "Unless I miss my guess, Oscar's got an accomplice we haven't met yet—somebody in the oil business."

"That's all great," Barbara said. "But you're forgetting something."

The Hardys looked at one another. "Forgetting what?" Joe asked.

"Jerry Greene." Barbara's face was somber. "It's beginning to sound to me as if Jerry might have stumbled onto their game. And if he did . . ."

Joe completed the sentence for her. "If he did, they probably finished him off." He stood up, too. "We've *got* to get back to the ranch and warn Roy. With this much at stake, there's no telling what these guys will do next."

Frank snapped back to their present bad situation. "Without water," he commented wryly, "one murder could easily turn into three more."

Barbara stood up. "Maybe we can still find some—yiii!" She slipped on a ridge of loose sand, sliding down hard into the ferny branches of a half-buried mesquite bush.

Joe followed her—more carefully—and helped Barbara back to her feet. But she limped as they stumbled over to Frank. "Oh, great," Barbara said, pointing at her leg with a grimace.

Joe looked—and sucked in a quick breath. Four ugly red blotches marred her khaki trouser leg—and sticking out of them were two-inch-long mesquite thorns.

"Broke my fall on a branch," she said in a

shaky voice. "But it got its revenge. I don't know how far I can walk just now."

Joe knelt down beside her. Together, they gently pulled the thorns free. Barbara rolled up the leg of the jumpsuit. The bleeding was already beginning to stop, but the areas around the wounds had turned an angry-looking red. They were also beginning to swell.

"Does it hurt?" Joe asked.

"Not too much yet," she said. "But it will." She stretched her leg out in front of her. "I won't be able to search—but one of you should check out the area for water. If we don't find any, I suggest that we just cool it here in the shade until the sun comes down." She glanced up at the sun again. "We'll stand a better chance of survival if we don't move around in this heat."

Frank and Joe flipped a coin, and Frank got the job. Half an hour later he returned from the search, looking hot and sweaty. Joe didn't envy him—the weather forecast had called for a high of 115 degrees.

Frank squatted down beside them. "I lost more water than I found," he said. "Looks like we don't have any other choice—we'll stay put until sunset." He shook his head.

An hour passed, then another, and another. The sun, burning orange in a sky of molten brass, crossed the zenith and began to fall toward the west. Even in the dusty shade of the mesquite, the temperature must have been well over a hundred. It felt like the inside of a kiln, a fierce, dry heat that seemed to warp the roof of Joe's mouth.

Even the flies were off somewhere taking a nap, Joe noticed almost in a daze. He saw lots of ants, though, and he could hear the erratic *click-click-click* of a locust on the bush above him. Far overhead, buzzards soared in expanding spirals, never in a hurry. Joe began to wonder if that wasn't quite a flock of them overhead, their wings like coal black *V*'s against the sky. What were they waiting for?

Suddenly Joe sat up. A movement in the brush had caught his eye.

"Ss-s-t." He leaned over and tapped Frank on the shoulder, pointing.

A figure lean and gaunt as a scarecrow stepped into the clearing. He wore homespun cotton pants and shirt. There was a straw hat on his head.

"It's Charlie!" Joe whispered. Beside Joe, Barbara stirred, sat up, and rubbed her eyes.

"What did I tell you?" Frank asked with a grin. "Didn't I say he'd show up again?"

The old man looked directly at them, beckoned slowly with one upraised hand, then turned and vanished into the brush again.

"I think he wants us to follow him," Frank said.

"But it looks like he's heading east," Joe

said uneasily. "We want to go *west*, toward the ranch."

Painfully, Barbara pushed herself up. "I'd bet on Charlie," she said. "His people lived on this land long before any of us got here. We can count on him to get us out of this fix."

Frank nodded. "Let's go," he said. With Barbara hobbling along, leaning on Joe for support, they made their way slowly after Charlie.

He glanced back at them, and motioned for them to stay low. A second later they saw a brief glint of light up on the caprock far to the east.

"I'll bet that's either a pair of binoculars or a rifle scope," Frank said, as they crouched down. "Our friends must be keeping an eye on us."

"That flash came from just south of Lawson's Bluff," Barbara said, a little breathlessly. "That's down on the Triple O."

"How come I'm not surprised?" Joe muttered.

A little farther on Charlie led them into a dry stream bed that wound eastward, toward the caprock. The gullied sides were just high enough to hide them from the bluff where the flash had come from. The ravine floor was littered with rocks and rough gravel, and in places it was crusted with white, sun-baked alkali. It was slow, hard going, but Joe had to admit it was better than being shot at.

He marveled at Charlie. The man's thin, wiry body moved effortlessly. He never glanced at the ground. Yet he put each foot down firmly and surely, without pausing, without stumbling, his sandals never leaving a print in the dusty sand. How did he do it? For a second Joe wondered if he were following a mirage. Then he grinned. "The heat must be getting to me," he told himself. "The three of us wouldn't see the same mirage."

To keep himself going, Joe began counting steps. When he reached a thousand, he glanced at Barbara. "How're you doing?" he asked. She'd managed to keep pace with him, but she was limping and leaning on him more and more heavily. He knew that leg must be giving her real trouble.

"I'll make it." She smiled bravely, but her dry lips had little cracks. "But I sure could use a drink of water. Anybody have a Popsicle?"

Joe laughed. He knew what she was talking about. His mouth was as dry as parched shoeleather, and he was beginning to feel a little lightheaded. Somewhere close by, a raven gave a loud, raucous laugh, and a minute later, a couple of other ravens joined him in a chorus of mad laughter.

Joe didn't blame them. There had to be something pretty funny about two greenhorns and a girl following a little old man down a bone-dry canyon under a blast-furnace sun. If his mouth weren't so dry, he'd laugh, too.

But he realized they were getting somewhere. Now the caprock cliff towered above them. Ahead, the dry stream bed they were following made a sharp bend around a heap of big gray boulders, fragments of the cliff face that had broken off and tumbled down. Beyond, Joe could see the green shadow of what looked like a cottonwood tree.

"I guess the heat's getting to me," Frank said. "I'd swear I just heard running water."

Joe and Barbara stopped and listened. The sound of the wind rose and fell, eerily, and Joe could hear the faraway call of a mourning dove. But beneath those sounds was an unmistakably melodious note—the sound of water dripping into a deep pool! Without a word, they redoubled their efforts to catch up with Charlie, who had never broken his effortless pace.

"Look!" Frank exclaimed, as they rounded the heap of boulders.

A clear ribbon of water oozed from a thin, crumbly layer of sediment in the cliff. It trickled over harder rock, then dropped six feet into a deeply sculptured basin in the rock below. The water hold was surrounded by monkey flowers and clumps of maidenhair ferns. Overhead the wind stirred the cool, green canopy of cottonwood.

Seconds later, as Charlie watched, the three of them lay flat on their faces, drinking the cool, sweet water. After he'd sipped enough, Joe dunked his head and shoulders under, staying a long time, letting the water cool him off.

"Watch out," Frank cautioned Joe when he finally came up for air. "You don't want to drown in the stuff."

"Drown?" Joe laughed, giving his head a shake. He took another loud slurp. "When I finish drinking, there won't be enough left to drown in."

"It's funny," Barbara said. "I've been all over this part of the cliff, and I didn't know this spring was here. It must be seasonal."

"I'm for staying until it dries up." Joe stretched out in the shade of the cottonwood.

"Where do you think we are?" Frank asked Barbara.

Barbara grinned. "You're not going to believe this, but I'll bet we're almost directly below the bunkhouse. It's on the caprock, up there."

At that moment Charlie stepped forward and said something to Barbara in what sounded to Joe like Spanish. She replied. Joe couldn't make out anything but the urgency in Charlie's voice.

"He says we have to go now," Barbara told them. "If we don't hurry, we'll be late."

"Late for what?" Joe demanded without

stirring. He opened his eyes. "Is somebody giving a party?"

"I couldn't quite make out why," Barbara replied. "But it's got something to do with getting to the top of the caprock."

Joe blinked. "Up *there?*" he asked. The top of the caprock was straight over their heads. "What does he think we are, mountain goats?"

But Charlie had already set off, taking a narrow path that clung to the side of the cliff.

Joe stood up with a sigh. He could take the climb, maybe. But what about Barbara?

She caught his look. "I can make it."

They climbed for a half hour. The sun was much lower in the west now and not so hot. But the loose limestone made the footing treacherous, and at its widest, the trail was only a foot wide. Ahead of them, Charlie moved along steadily, never wavering. Behind him, Barbara faltered, clinging to the rock with both hands. Joe and Frank brought up the rear, moving carefully, one foot in front of the other. Joe didn't want to look down.

When they finally reached the top, they were only a hundred yards from the bunkhouse. Bringing up the rear, Frank breathed a sigh of relief and took a quick look around. Everything was quiet. More importantly, the pickup truck was still parked beside the house, still in one piece.

Charlie picked up the pace now, heading

straight for the house. When they'd gotten almost to the back door, Frank turned to Joe. "You don't suppose we're walking into another trap, do you?"

Joe looked around carefully. "He could have left us out on the sand," he said. "But he got us here safely. I'd trust him a little further."

Charlie was saying something to Barbara.

"He wants us to go in," she said. "He says we've got to hurry."

Frank stepped to the kitchen window, checking the inside of the small house. "Everything seems okay," he said. "Just the way we left it this morning." He opened the back door.

"I still don't understand," Joe said as he stepped in. "Why all the hurry? What's—"

"Telephone!" Charlie said in a low voice, raising his hand to his ear as if he were picking up the receiver.

Pick up the phone? Was that what Charlie wanted? Frowning, Frank reached for the receiver.

"Careful!" Charlie whispered, putting his finger to his lips.

Gently, Frank lifted the receiver, keeping a hand over the mouthpiece.

"Told you . . . never use . . . party line . . . risky!" The line crackled with static, and the angry voice was too low-pitched to make everything out.

"Relax, relax," another voice said. Maybe it

was nearer, because it came through a little more clearly. Frank wished the line were better—he almost recognized the speaker. "The only other phone on this line is Carlson's bunkhouse. And I left those kids in a bad way. The sun's probably finished them off by now." A blast of static cut him off in midlaugh.

Frank picked up the conversation again. "Greene kid played his part well . . . wait for the two of you up here on the caprock."

Another blast of static wiped out the response. "Reach the old windmill to pick up our other friend. Look for us after dark."

Frank had to strain to hear the next part. But what he caught made his stomach turn over. "Have two bodies to get rid of instead of one."

Chapter 14

FRANK HEARD A LOUD CLICK, and the connection was broken. He put the receiver down and faced the others. "I wish that line had been better. I knew the voice, but couldn't swear it was Owens. At least it confirms part of our suspicions—there is an accomplice involved." He shook his head. "But from the sound of things, Jerry's mixed up in it, too."

Barbara shook her head firmly. "I can't believe that Jerry's part of this," she protested. "He's just not the kind of guy to—"

"Look!" Joe exclaimed. "He's done it again!"

Frank turned. Joe was pointing to the open door. Charlie was nowhere to be seen.

"We turn our back on him for one second," Joe said, "and he goes into his vanishing act."

"I guess he figures we can take it from here." Frank grinned crookedly. "I hope he's right."

"Listen," Joe said, leaning forward, "I'm with Barbara on this Jerry bit. She knows him—we don't."

Frank nodded. "It did sound as if the guy on the other end was on his way to pick somebody up. And if they're planning to kill two people, that must mean Jerry and this other person. We need to get to Roy," Frank said urgently. "They talked about an 'old windmill,' and maybe Roy knows what they might have been talking about. It sounded as if they were on the caprock somewhere."

"We don't dare phone him, though," Joe said. "The bad guys might pick us up on the party line. We've got the old yellow pickup, but it doesn't have a CB." He looked at Barbara. "We used the ranch road to get here. Is there a faster way back to the Circle C ranch house?"

"The long way round, by the highway," Barbara replied. "It's probably ten miles farther, but it's a lot faster and there's less risk of being spotted."

Frank and Joe checked out the pickup in record time.

"It looks like you guys have had a lot of practice at this," Barbara said as Joe rolled under the pickup and Frank crawled under the dashboard.

"You bet," Joe told her. "As of a couple of days ago, we don't drive *anything* we haven't checked out first."

"Clear here," Frank called.

"Let's go," Joe said, sliding into the driver's seat. "Roll 'em!" He shoved the gearstick into first, scattering gravel, and they were off.

They were a mile and a half from the ranch house when a sharp *bang* came from the right front. The truck pulled hard to the right. Wrestling the wheel, Joe managed to keep the truck from skidding and bring it to a smooth stop on the shoulder.

"Of all the luck!" Joe thundered. "A blowout! Just what we need!" He thumped the steering wheel.

Frank peered around cautiously. There wasn't any good cover nearby. "You don't suppose somebody took a shot at us, do you?"

Joe was already out of the truck, studying the flat tire. "Doesn't look like it to me. I think we just got unlucky." He stood up, scowling. "Now what?"

Frank looked in the bed of the truck and gave the spare tire a thump with his fist. "Looks like the spare's good, and there's a jack behind the seat. I'll take off on foot, and we'll see who's fastest."

"I'd race you, but . . ." Barbara gave a wan smile at her injured leg.

"I'll need someone to cheer me on with this tire fixing," Joe said with a grin.

Frank set off at an even, steady trot. It was much cooler now that it was almost sunset, and the sun was falling into a cloud bank of crimson and orange and blue. A nighthawk, high above, folded its wings and plunged straight down through the still air, pulling up just above Frank's head, where it plucked an insect out of the air and soared away.

Fifteen minutes after he'd left Joe, Frank panted the last hundred feet up to the ranch house. The only vehicle he could see out front was the white car that Dot drove. Shep came running out to greet him with a storm of excited barks. Dot came out on the front porch.

"Frank!" she exclaimed. "What are you doing on foot? Where's Joe?"

"Fixing a flat," Frank gasped, catching his breath. "They'll be along in a minute." He stepped up onto the porch. "Where's Roy? I need to talk to him right away. We've solved the case! Now all we have to do is find Jerry and—"

"Find Jerry?" Dot broke in, looking confused. "But I don't understand. Roy's already left, to meet *you*. Right after he got the phone call, three-quarters of an hour ago."

Frank stopped dead still. "To meet *us?* Who called?"

Dot's confusion was turning to concern. "Roy didn't know who it was. Anyway, whoever it was said that Jerry was still alive and that you and Joe had found out where he was. Roy was suspicious—he insisted on talking to Jerry in person."

"What happened then?" Frank asked. He could see a cloud of dust on the road, the yellow pickup barreling in front of it.

"Then Jerry came on the line and said he was okay. Roy was sure that it was Jerry's voice, even though he sounded like he was sort of in a daze." She stopped, her voice beginning to fill with panic. "After that, the caller came back on the line. He said—he said that he had you and Joe and Jerry, and that if Roy wanted to see any of you alive again, he had to meet him. Right away. Alone."

"Meet him *where?*" Frank demanded. But he already knew the answer.

"At the windmill," Dot replied. "Down on the old homestead."

Frank kept his face still. How was he going to tell Dot that Roy's appointment was a setup for murder?

Chapter 15

"BAD NEWS!" Frank shouted as Joe drove up. "They're after Roy. He left for the old homestead nearly an hour ago."

"Roy Carlson!" Barbara exclaimed. Then she nodded. "That figures, I guess."

"What are we waiting for?" Joe demanded. He put the truck into reverse and got ready to back up. "Let's go! Maybe we can get there in time."

Frank shook his head. Whatever was planned at the old windmill had already happened. Joe cut the engine in disgust. But from the look on Frank's face, they might have another plan.

"It'll be dark in half an hour," Frank told them. "Owens said that he and Jerry would be waiting up on the caprock. So that's where this other guy will be taking Roy. They've counted us out. So if we can get up there, maybe we can catch them off guard—and save Roy and Jerry."

"But *where* on the caprock?" Barbara wondered.

Frank wheeled to face Dot. "We're looking for a place that's on the same party line as the bunkhouse," he said.

Dot's face was drawn with worry. "Then you're looking for the old shack at the north end of the Triple O, just south of Lawson's Bluff. The place is a wreck—I thought that phone line had been down for years."

"Well, that explains the great connection on the call we overheard," Frank said.

"And that must have been where we saw the flash this afternoon," Barbara added.

"How's the land there?" Frank asked. "Flat and fairly open, like around the bunkhouse?"

Dot frowned. "As best I can recall, it's mostly open pasture with some mesquite bushes. There's an old shed and a corral out back. And it's quite a distance from the highway."

Joe leaned against the truck. "They're bound to be keeping an eye on the road coming in from the highway," he said, "so we can't surprise them that way." He shook his head. "Too bad we don't have more time. We could cross the sand hills and climb the caprock, the way we did this afternoon."

"Yeah, sure," Barbara said skeptically. "In the dark, without Charlie to guide us."

"Anyway, there's no time for that, even if we could," Frank said. He grinned. "What I had in mind was dropping in on them."

Without waiting to explain, he strode into the house and headed for the office, where he studied the wall map for a minute, and then got a ruler out of the desk and began to measure distances on the map. Finally, he sat at the desk and began to punch numbers into the calculator. "It should work," he muttered to himself, satisfied. When he came back out onto the porch, Barbara and Dot were talking in low voices, confusion on their faces. Joe was wearing a big grin.

"*Drop in* on them?" Dot asked. "What in the world are you talking about, Frank?"

Frank pointed toward the east. Above the caprock, slightly to the north, they could see some blinking red lights.

"Those lights mark three tall radio towers a couple of miles beyond the caprock," he said. "If Joe and I fly directly toward them—"

Barbara gave Frank a withering look. "And just where are you planning to get your wings, Peter Pan?"

Frank ignored her. "If we fly directly toward them in the ultralight, we'll get to maximum altitude just as we cross the caprock. From that point, we should be able to reach our objective."

"But that contraption makes too much noise," Joe objected. "They'll hear us coming and shoot us out of the sky."

Frank grinned. "There won't *be* any noise. When we cross the caprock, we cut the engine and glide the rest of the way. I figured it out on the calculator. At maximum altitude, and with the ultralight's glide ratio, we can make it to the shack where they're holed up."

Joe stared at him. *"Glide?"* He gulped.

Frank paused, testing the wind. The crescent moon was just rising to the south of the radio towers.

"Unfortunately, this south wind isn't going to help. It'll cut our ground speed. But the moon should give us enough light to spot the shack from the air, even if they don't have any lights on."

"Assuming you find it," Barbara asked worriedly, "what then?"

Frank squared his shoulders. "The tough part is the landing. We'll have only one try. If we have to restart the engine, they'll hear us. And then we might as well forget rescuing Roy and Jerry."

"What can *we* do?" Dot asked.

"You and Barbara can get ahold of Sheriff Clinton and seal off the road," Frank said. "In fact, you might even catch the guy who's bringing Roy in." He chewed his lip. "I just hope he hasn't got there yet with Roy. I have the feeling that Roy and Jerry won't stay alive very long once they're up there."

"What if you need reinforcements?" Barbara asked.

"We'll signal. Three of anything—shots, honks, flashes," Frank said. "That'll be your signal to close in."

While Dot began to dial the phone, Frank, Joe, and Barbara headed for the barn and rolled the ultralight outside.

"We'd better top off the tank," Frank told Joe. "Running out of gas tonight could be embarrassing."

Barbara picked up a gas can inside the door and followed them as they pushed the ultralight onto the dirt road. She was still limping. Frank took the can and filled the small fuel tank.

"I think that does it." He stepped beside the pilot's seat.

Joe looked at the light craft. Suddenly, it seemed pretty puny looking.

"What did you say the maximum altitude is?" he asked, trying to keep the uneasiness out of his voice.

"About five thousand feet," Frank replied carelessly, climbing in. He was grinning. "Come on. No guts, no glory!" He turned on the ignition, and the little engine screamed to life.

"Take care, cowboy." Barbara gave Joe a quick hug. Then Joe climbed in beside Frank, trying not to look as reluctant as he felt.

"Are we legal?" he shouted, over the shrill whine of the engine.

"Not until I get my license," Frank replied, testing the controls. "If we run into an FAA inspector, you'll have to get out and walk." He stared into Joe's unhappy face. "Look, it's the only way we can get there to save Jerry and Roy."

The yellow pickup rolled to a stop beside the ultralight and Barbara ran over to it. Dot took a shotgun out of the gun rack and handed it to Barbara through the window, saying something Joe couldn't hear.

"Dot says you might need this," Barbara reported, handing Joe the gun. "Just in case you run into varmints or something."

Joe gave her a thumbs-up as Frank pushed the throttle to full power. The ultralight gained speed very slowly, it seemed to Joe. Finally, Frank eased the controls back and slowly, laboriously, they rose into the air.

"Anybody ever tell you that you're a lot of dead weight?" Frank shouted as they sluggishly climbed above the scrub.

"I just hope you did those calculations

right," Joe said with a worried glance groundward.

He could see the lights of the pickup already heading north at top speed toward the highway. Ahead of them in the darkness were the three radio towers, their red lights blinking. Frank turned the ultralight to bear directly on them and leveled the wings. Slowly they gained altitude, climbing through the chilly dusk, the laboring engine shrieking in Joe's ears.

"With this load," Frank shouted, "we won't make much better time than they will in the pickup, even if we are cutting cross-country."

Joe nodded. The ground below them was rapidly losing its landmarks in the darkness. Here and there a light patch of sandy dune stood out. The moon still hung low on the horizon. Somehow, those three strings of red lights straight ahead gave Joe a lot of comfort. Then, after a little while, he saw the caprock cliff below, a long, chalk-white thread that wound across the darkness below. From five thousand feet, it looked tiny—nothing at all like the frightening cliff they'd climbed just that afternoon.

At that moment Frank pulled back on the throttle. The engine cut off, leaving a high-pitched ringing in Joe's ears. The only other sounds were the rush of air over the surface of the wings and the eerie whistle of the wind through the struts.

"Here goes." Frank banked the ultralight to the right, heading south.

Now they were slipping effortlessly through the darkness, losing altitude in a long, smooth glide. Frank leveled the wings. "Five minutes to touchdown," he said. "Watch for the shack—and keep your eyes peeled for a good landing zone."

So this is what the glider troops in World War Two felt like, Joe thought. There was a knot in the pit of his stomach and his mouth was dry. He remembered reading that some of those night operations had been real disasters—gliders piling up against trees and fences. He'd always trusted his brother to get them out of tight spots—but *this* was a killer!

They were near enough to the ground so that Joe could begin to make out surface features in the dim moonlight. There were open areas which appeared to be covered with grass, broken with shadowy spots that might be mesquite. Occasionally, the shadowy splotches seemed very dense. Joe shuddered as he thought of those mesquite thorns, sharp as needles, hard as nails.

"Lawson's Bluff coming up," Frank said, pointing ahead and to the right, where the caprock jutted out. It was bare and open but not level enough for a landing, Joe saw. On its far side was the line traced by a barbed wire fence. Briefly, he wondered what the Native

Americans would have thought, the night of the raid, if a strange machine like this one had dropped in on them from the sky.

"Hey, a light!" Joe exclaimed, pointing to a single pinprick of yellow, two hundred yards ahead of them. Then, in the moonlight, he began to pick out the structures—a small cabin, with corrals and a shed behind it.

"We need a landing spot, in a *hurry,*" Frank said, his voice grimly urgent.

Joe was suddenly aware that every inch of ground beneath them was covered with dense growth and the shadows it cast.

Off to the left he spotted a patch of what looked like open pasture. "How about there?" he said, pointing.

Frank banked the ultralight and headed for it. But then Joe could see that the shadows were lengthening out ahead of them. The open patch had disappeared behind clumps of brush and trees.

Frank's voice was tight. "We're not going to make it."

Chapter 16

THE DARK, SCRAWNY SHAPES of bushes seemed to rush up at them. "Hang on tight," Frank said. "We're going in!"

As they began to slice through the feathery tops of the mesquite, Frank pulled back on the controls. The nose of the ultralight rose, almost hanging in front of them. Then the craft seemed to drop out from underneath them. Joe felt it shudder as the limbs caught at it, then gave way under its weight, crackling sharply. The front tire hit the ground, but the steel tube that supported it bent. They thumped to the ground.

Joe was tossed forward to bounce against his seat belt. The ultralight leaned crazily, its rear wheels still caught in the bushes. The shotgun fell out.

"You all right?" Joe asked, turning to Frank.

"Somebody said any landing you can walk away from is a good landing," Frank replied, undoing his seat belt. "Let's see about that."

As Joe gingerly climbed out, he stubbed his toe against something. He looked down to find the missing shotgun. Its butt stock was snapped at the neck. The gun was worthless.

The Hardys made their way through the mesquite to the clearing where they'd seen the light. A shadowy figure stood on the rickety front porch, looking toward them. At that moment, a bull in the pasture behind them gave a loud bellow. The figure on the porch turned back into the house.

"Think he heard anything?" Joe whispered.

"Probably. But he must have thought it was the cattle, crashing through the brush." Frank shrugged. "I guess we're lucky there's a lot of mesquite between here and where we landed."

They waited a couple of minutes, but there was no move from the cabin. The sounds of country and western music drifted out of a window into the cool night air.

"Well, if we want something to happen, looks like it's up to us to *make* it happen," Frank whispered. "Here's what I suggest."

Joe listened, then nodded. "Gotcha."

A moment later Frank darted across the dusty, rock-littered yard, keeping low and in the shadows. He reached the porch and crouched down.

"Hey, Jerry!" he heard Joe shout, from his concealed position.

The radio suddenly clicked off and the light went out. Frank heard the sound of heavy feet running across a wooden floor and a screen door screeching open and slamming shut. Footsteps pounded the porch and the wooden steps as a figure with a drawn revolver charged past.

Frank lunged in a diving tackle. Smashing into the guy, he was a little surprised—Oscar Owens was fairly short. The figure that toppled to the ground was huge. At least the gun flew from the guy's hand to land with a thud in the soft dust several feet away.

The man made a quick recovery, scrambling to his feet to face off against Frank. It was Nat Wilkin! Frank froze in an instant of surprise—and Nat took advantage of it. A giant fist came like a pile driver toward Frank's jaw. Frank managed to divert the blow but not the momentum of the charging figure behind it. Nat ran full into Frank, knocking him flat on his back, then he crashed down on top of him.

A blow from that iron fist slammed into the side of Frank's head. He shook his head, trying to clear his eyes—and wished he hadn't. A large hunk of limestone in two giant hands hovered over his head. Nat knelt over him with an evil grin, ready to smash the rock into his face. Frank could hardly move, much yet fend him off.

"Freeze!" The command seemed faint, far away.

But the rock hesitated over him.

"Don't even think about it." The voice came closer. "Put it down. Very gently." The voice was harsh. "This is no time for a mistake."

The rock came to rest on the ground, inches from Frank's face.

Now Frank saw the barrel of a very large pistol jabbing Nat just behind his right ear. The pistol was held in Joe's strong, steady grasp.

"Lace your fingers behind your head," Joe commanded. "Get up—slowly."

Nat was red-faced with rage. "I'll have you punks tossed into the pen!" he snarled, glaring at Joe. "Trespassing and assault!"

Joe faced him calmly. "I'll see that and raise you two counts of kidnapping and three counts of attempted murder."

"That wasn't my idea!" Nat whined. Then he checked himself.

Frank got to his feet. "Maybe you'd like to tell us whose idea it was," he suggested, brushing himself off.

"I bet you'd like that," Nat growled. "But the game's not over."

Frank nodded. "The rest of the players haven't shown up yet, have they?" He stepped onto the porch. An ancient bell hung there—

rusty, but loud enough when he gave the warning signal.

Bong! Bong! Bong! The three deep notes reverberated through the still night air.

"Let's have a look inside." Joe prodded Nat forward at pistol point.

Frank turned on the light inside the door. A young man lay on a bunk, his eyes glazed. Frank knelt beside the bunk to check Jerry's pulse. "What did you do to him?" he demanded.

"Hey, nothing," Nat said, shifting nervously away from Joe. "Nothing a little sleep won't cure, anyway." He shuddered. "Be careful with that gun, kid. It's got a hair trigger."

Frank heard the sound of the two vehicles coming up, and glanced out the window. "Here comes our reinforcements," he confirmed to Joe. Two pairs of parking lights bounced swiftly through the pasture to the east. In the moonlight Frank recognized the yellow pickup, leading a squad car. He stepped to the porch and waved.

"Frank! Where's Joe?" Barbara called, jumping out of the truck even before it rolled to a stop.

"He's inside." Frank grinned. "Keeping tabs on Nat Wilkin, of all people. And we've got Jerry, too," he added as Dot came running up. "I think he's going to be okay."

Dot was followed by a stern-faced Sheriff Clinton. "What's going on here?"

"Kidnapping, for starters," Frank told him.

The sheriff stepped past Frank, into the room. While Joe still kept the prisoner covered, Clinton pulled Nat's hands down, one at a time, and deftly handcuffed them behind his back.

"What about Roy?" Dot asked worriedly.

"We haven't seen him," Frank said. "What about you? Did you see anything out there?"

"Not a thing." Dot sounded scared. "Oh, Frank, what if Roy's already—"

"Well, Nat," the sheriff said, pushing Wilkin out onto the porch. "What have you got to say for yourself?"

Nat didn't reply. He seemed to be listening. Then an unpleasant smile spread over his face.

Barbara turned, looking toward the west. "What's that sound?" she whispered, as Joe came out onto the porch behind her.

They all heard it now—a roaring rumble like a monster engine, protesting under a heavy load. The sound came from below the cliff.

"I'd say," Frank remarked, "that it's a very large truck, in very low gear."

The noise grew rapidly louder, and the engine wound itself into a high-pitched whine. A squat, heavy shadow lumbered like a tank over the edge of the cliff. Frank recognized it immediately—it was the giant Mack truck cab that had nearly driven them off the road. Its lights were off. The moonlight reflected off the broad windshield and tall chrome grill. Then the headlights flashed twice and the engine was switched off.

"That must be some kind of signal," Joe said to Frank. "He must be expecting a countersign. But what?"

"The bell, maybe?" Frank replied.

They all turned to look at Nat. He just grinned at them.

"Well, now," he drawled. "It looks like you boys have run smack into a Mexican standoff!"

Chapter 17

NAT SQUARED OFF against them. In spite of the handcuffs on his wrists, he acted as if he were holding all the aces.

"Look, Sheriff, be reasonable," Nat said smoothly. "There's no point in anybody getting hurt, is there? We can do a deal here—you get Roy, and my friend and I get on our way."

"No way," Joe snapped.

"If anybody gets hurt," Frank said grimly, "*you're* an accomplice."

Their voices were drowned out as the truck engine started up, bringing the cab closer. Sheriff Clinton brought up a six-cell flashlight, shining it toward the truck.

"Wilkin! What do you think you're doing?" a furious voice came from the truck cab. Then everyone on the porch was blinded as the truck's huge lights came on, dazzling them.

"Looks like you really fouled things up, huh, Nat? Sheriff, you've got Nat, and as far as I'm concerned, you can keep him. I just want to get out of here."

"What makes you think we'll let you get away?" the sheriff shouted.

The voice chuckled. "Because I've got insurance, that's why." The truck door slammed open. "His name is Roy Carlson!" Against the glare of the high beams, they saw the shadowy form of a tall man, hands crossed in front of him. A shorter, stockier figure prodded him along with a long-barreled weapon.

"That's Roy!" Dot whispered. "What are we going to do?"

Nat spit into the dust. "That no-good double-crossing snake," he muttered. "I knew he was crazy, but I thought I could trust him."

Abruptly, the short, stocky man pushed Roy forward a few paces. Roy stumbled and caught himself.

"Look, people, what's it going to be?" the voice demanded. Against the lights, they saw the rifle come up. "You've got ten seconds! Let me go, or I'll blast good old Roy!"

Frank and Joe stared at each other helplessly. Silence hung over the scene, while the crescent moon cast long, strange shadows over the pasture, the corral, and the bluff beyond.

"One," the shadowy figure called out. "Two—three—"

"You think he means it?" Sheriff Clinton asked Nat.

"He's got nothing to lose," Wilkin said worriedly. He'd just realized that he was the one who'd be paying if Roy got killed.

"Five—six—seven," the gunman's voice counted out.

Beside them, Dot Carlson began to whimper.

"Eight—"

"Stop it! Stop it!" Dot screamed. "Let my husband go!"

Clinton looked helplessly from Dot to the two figures outlined against the lights.

"Nine—te—"

The voice cut off as another sound broke in—a rattling that was quiet, but grew louder. The stocky figure in front of the truck whirled around.

"Hey-hey-hey-ya! Hey-hey-hey-ya!" A thin, wavering chant rose rhythmically into the moonlight, bone-chilling, bloodcurdling. Beyond the truck, on the other side of the fence that ran beside the promontory of Lawson's Bluff, a skeletal apparition rose up, arms extended to the open sky. "Hey-ya-hey-ya-hey!" The apparition turned several times, bending and bowing in a slow dance.

"You there! You stop that!" the stocky man commanded. He stepped toward the dancer, his attention momentarily diverted from Roy and the group on the porch.

"Come on," Joe whispered, grabbing Frank's arm. "Let's circle around behind the corral!" The two boys slipped into the cover of the shadows and began making their way silently toward the corral.

"Hey-hey-hey-ya!" The thin, tuneless chant came again, fading, then growing louder.

"That's got to be Charlie out there," Frank whispered. "Boy, he sure turns up at the weirdest times."

Charlie's chanting was obviously getting on the stocky man's nerves. "Knock it off!" he yelled, backing that demand up with a wild shot.

The boys reached the corner of the corral and peeked around it. The stocky man had turned his back on Roy. He was concentrating on the dancing figure, now beginning to circle on the rock, with a slow, shuffling step.

The pitch of the chant rose and the speed picked up as the figure swayed and turned, faster and faster. Joe had to admit that the dance was eerie, frightening. It was like a ghost dancing out there—the ghost of the long-dead Native Americans who had once ruled this cliff, this desert.

"Hey-hey-hey, hey-hey-hey, hey-ya, hey-ya!"

"Stop!" The stocky man had vaulted the

fence that separated him from Charlie. He was advancing on the dancer, the barrel of his gun pointed menacingly.

Roy took advantage of his captor's distraction, stumbling as he ran for the safety of the corral.

"Over here, Roy!" Frank called, in a low voice. In a second Roy was beside them and they were untying his hands.

"Boy, am I glad to see you guys," Roy said, rubbing his wrists. "That guy—the guy driving the truck—he's nuts. I thought I was a goner for sure." He peered in the direction of the dancer. "What's going on out there?"

They were close enough to make out the scene clearly. Charlie was moving faster and faster, his chant rising in a wild wail. His long hair was woven into braids, and he held something in his hand, something that twisted and writhed.

"It's a *snake!*" Joe gasped. "He's got a live snake out there!"

Frank shook his head. "Risky business, if you ask me."

"Hey-ya-hey-ya-HI!"

Facing the man with the gun, Charlie suddenly stood tall and flung his arms wide.

"Get it away!" the man shouted, his gun sailing as he leaped away. A second later, he was on his knees. "My leg! Help! I've been snake bit! A rattler got me!"

In an instant Frank and Joe were over the fence. They seized the man and dragged him to his feet, searching him quickly. He had no weapons, but in his pocket Frank found a handful of blasting caps.

"Like to play with these, huh?" Frank murmured.

"I need a doctor," the man said. There was panic in his voice. He looked down at his leg. "I need a doctor, *bad!*"

Frank and Joe sat him down. Joe removed one of his shoe laces and began tying it tight around the leg, just above the bite. "You'll live," he said. "Probably."

Frank nudged Joe. "Hey," he said, "he's done it again."

Joe straightened up, pulling the stocky man upright. "Who?"

"Charlie."

Frank pointed. All of Lawson's Bluff lay still and empty. Charlie and his snake had vanished.

Chapter 18

"BARBARA'S LATE," Joe complained with a look at his watch. He was sitting on the tailgate of the old yellow pickup, parked in front of the Circle C ranch house.

Frank stood beside their luggage. "I can't believe you're in such a big hurry to get out of here." He grinned at Joe. "I thought you'd miss Barbara."

Joe shrugged, a little embarrassed. "You've got to admit she was pretty nice, offering to drive us all the way back to Lubbock Airport."

"It was the least she could do," Frank pointed out, "after we sweated all morning in the mesquite, changing Tinkerbell's radiator." He laughed. "We saved Barb a humongous towing bill—and Tinkerbell a very uncomfortable trip."

Roy Carlson came out of the ranch house, a happy smile on his face. "Sorry I wasn't able to say goodbye before. I was on the phone to the hospital—just talked to Jerry, and he sounds super. The doc doesn't think he'll suffer any permanent effects from that stuff those guys doped him with. But he wants to keep an eye on him for a couple of days."

"How about Nat and his partner?" Frank asked. "Have they started talking yet?"

"It's amazing how a night in jail—or in the hospital—can make a fella talk," Roy said. "I got an earful from Bobby Clinton while you boys were out fixing Barbara's jeep."

"Do we know who that guy in the truck was?" Joe asked.

"His name is John Hicks," Roy said. "That sidewinder bite made him pretty sick—and scared. He told Bobby his whole life story. Apparently, Hicks worked for a few oil companies, long enough to pick up some of the basics about oil exploration. He learned how to handle explosives in the army."

Roy shook his head. "Believe it or not, his people came from around here."

The Hardys stared as the rancher went on.

"The Hicks family homesteaded in this area, back when the original oil survey was made, more than fifty years back. They went bust, but there was some kind of family legend about their being cheated out of the land and the oil under it.''

Roy sighed. ''Seems Hicks was telling the story one night in a bar and Nat overheard. He figured if the story turned out to be true, there was a lot of money to be made. So they formed a partnership of sorts.''

Joe shook his head. ''I think Nat got more than he bargained for. Hicks is more than a little crazy.''

Frank nodded. ''From the way they acted last night, those two looked ready to kill each other.''

''Nat's already talked his head off,'' Roy agreed. ''So Bobby's got a pretty good idea of what happened. Old Nat went off and got the mineral leases for the federal land. But they wanted me off so I wouldn't find out what they were up to. Wilkin and Hicks set out to make ranching that land real unprofitable—they figured I'd decide not to renew my grazing lease.''

''That was probably after they'd started the seismographic tests, and figured out about the salt dome,'' Frank said. ''They knew most of the oil was on Roy's property, so they were doing the final tests to figure where to drill and siphon off the oil.''

''And Jerry caught them in the act,'' Joe said.

''That's right,'' Roy told them. ''They

grabbed him, then panicked and stashed him in that abandoned shack. Turned his horse loose in the sand hills to make it look like he was thrown."

"I guess they were afraid I'd see their test holes when I flew over in the ultralight that first day, looking for Jerry," Frank said. "That's when Nat took a shot at me with the three-oh-three, cutting the rudder cable."

Roy nodded. "After that, they decided to lay low for a couple of days, until the heat was off. But they were pressed for time—Hicks was setting up a deal with a wildcat oil company to get in there and start stealing the oil."

"So, when Nat heard that the search was called off, they set off their last test?" Joe said.

"Right," Frank said. "We heard the blast, and thought it was thunder, but Hicks got it into his head that we were onto them and decided to eliminate us."

"That explains the dynamite in the stove, and the bomb in the truck." Joe shuddered. "He came pretty close, didn't he?"

"Let's not forget that near miss in the truck, on the road to Charlie's," Frank told him. "What I'd like to know, though, was how Charlie figured in all this."

"His main concern seems to have been that sacred place of his up on the caprock," Roy said. "Well, he doesn't need to worry about that as long as I'm alive. I plan to fence it off and leave it to him and his people."

Frank gave him an appraising look. "And what about the oil? What are you going to do about that?"

Roy stroked his chin. "Haven't decided yet. It's been there millions of years. And as far as I'm concerned, it can stay there a while longer." He scowled. "I don't like the idea of a bunch of oil patchers running all over my land, digging it up, fouling what little water we've got, scaring the cows, busting down the fences." He grinned crookedly. "Speaking of fences, I've got a few to mend myself—with Owens."

At that moment, Joe heard the blare of a jeep horn and a cloud of dust appeared over the ridge, trailing a candy-apple-colored jeep.

"Here comes Tinkerbell," he said with a grin.

Roy stuck out his hand. "Come back during hunting season if you like. Give my best to Charlie if you run into him, and tell him he's got nothing to worry about. And thanks again for everything. Have a good trip home."

The boys loaded their luggage into the jeep, and the three of them took off.

Barbara's long dark hair was flying in the breeze as she drove along the road. "Sorry I'm late, guys," she said.

"I didn't much mind," Frank said. "But Joe was getting a little antsy."

The look Joe gave his brother could have reduced him to a cinder. He still hadn't come up with anything to say when Tinkerbell rolled quietly into Charlie's yard. The old man was dozing in the sun near his front door, his hat pulled down over his eyes. When he heard the jeep, he rose slowly to meet them.

"Tell him what Roy said about the sacred land," Joe urged Barbara.

In a warm and gentle voice, Barbara began to speak to the old man in Spanish. His face remained expressionless, but there was a light in his eyes. When she finished, he replied with a few soft phrases.

"He says to thank Senor Roy for his understanding," she said. "He says it is good when people understand one another."

"I guess you can't expect him to say, 'thank you' for something that's already his," Joe said with a shrug.

"But we can say thanks to him for all the help he gave us," Frank said. "We wouldn't be around if it weren't for him.

Barbara translated, and Charlie gave them a slight smile.

"Ask him why he didn't tell us more the first night," Frank asked. "He could have saved us some digging."

Barbara spoke to the old man briefly, and he replied.

"He says he didn't know who you were at first. You might have been evil."

"How did he know about the other things?" Joe demanded. "The telephone call, for instance." He shook his head. "That was *weird.*"

Barbara spoke to him again.

This time, the old man only smiled broadly.

Frank and Joe's next case:

The Hardys investigate a curious series of gangland killings. Crime kingpin Josh Moran is dead and buried, but his murderous legacy lives on. In his will, he left $10 million to be divided among his enemies. The catch is that the money will be paid in three months—to those who survive.

Frank and Joe find themselves in a deadly race against time, for one of the beneficiaries of Moran's blood money is a former detective for the NYPD—their own father, Fenton Hardy. The brother detectives must unmask the triggerman before the dead man's hit list reaches into their own family . . . in *Blood Money,* Case #32 in The Hardy Boys Casefiles™.